The smell of arsenic lingers in the air...

Mind where you step, Maggie. These stairs are tricky, like everything else round this place. The wood's been scalloped by thousands of boots and slippers. Slave brogans and moccasins, too. People come from all over to gawk at Charles Willson Peale's pile of dead animals. "Great School of Nature!" he called his museum. Boastful old man.

MARY E. LYONS

the

Poison

A NOVEL

Place

ALADDIN PAPERBACKS

To the memory of Sima Beth Goodhartz

First Aladdin Paperbacks edition August 1999

Text copyright © 1997 by Mary E. Lyons

Aladdin Paperbacks
An imprint of Simon & Schuster Children's Publishing Division
1230 Avenue of the Americas
New York, NY 10020

Also available in an Atheneum Books for
Young Readers hardcover edition.
The text of this book was set in 11-point Horley Old Style.
Printed and bound in the United States of America
10 9 8 7 6 5 4 3 2 1

The Library of Congress has cataloged the hardcover
edition as follows:
Lyons, Mary E.
The poison place / Mary E. Lyons.
p. cm.
Summary: A former slave named Moses reminisces about his
famous owner, Charles Willson Peale, and the intrigue
surrounding Peale's son's suspicious death.
ISBN 0-689-81146-2 (hc.)
1. Peale, Charles Willson, 1741–1827—Juvenile fiction.
2. William, Moses, 1776–1833—Juvenile fiction.
[1. Peale, Charles Willson, 1741–1827—Fiction.
2. William, Moses, 1776–1833—Fiction. 3. Slavery—Fiction.
4. United States—History—Fiction.] I. Title
PZ7.L99556Po 1997
[Fic]—dc21
96-53678
ISBN 0-689-82678-8 (pbk.)

Contents

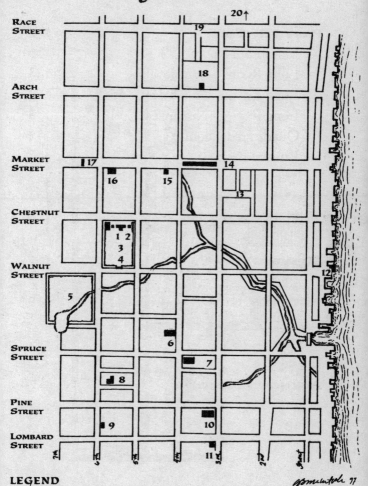

Map of Philadelphia

RACE STREET

ARCH STREET

MARKET STREET

CHESTNUT STREET

WALNUT STREET

SPRUCE STREET

PINE STREET

LOMBARD STREET

LEGEND

1. State House
2. Philosophical Hall
3. State House Yard
4. Walnut Street Gate to Yard
5. Potter's Field
6. St Mary's Catholic Church
7. Almshouse
8. Raphaelle Peale's House
9. Mother Bethel AME Church
10. St Peter's Anglican Church
11. Charles Willson Peale's House
12. Mullen's Dock
13. Elbow Lane
14. Covered Market
15. Black Bear Inn
16. President's Mansion
17. Triumphal Arch
18. St George's Methodist Church
19. Sterling Alley
20. Peg's Run Creek

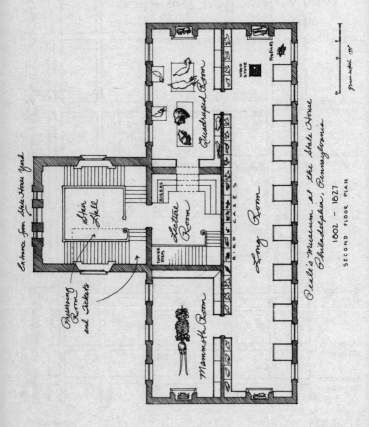

Entrance from State House Yard

Receiving Room and Toilets

Stair Hall

Tower Steps

Lecture Room

Mammoth Room

BIRD CASES

Quadruped Room

WOOD STOVE

PROFILES

Long Room

Peale's Museum at the State House
Philadelphia, Pennsylvania

1802 — 1827

SECOND FLOOR PLAN

**WHY DO THE VAIN AND EMPTY
EMPLOYMENTS OF LIFE TAKE
SUCH VAST HOLD ON US?**

from "A Prayer for Faith," circa 1787
Richard Allen, founder,
Mother Bethel Church,
Philadelphia, Pennsylvania

The Poison Place:

Memories of a Philadelphia Slave

Events in the life of Moses Williams
as told to his daughter Maggie;
Peale's Museum, Philadelphia, Pennsylvania;
February 22, 1827

Part I: ENTER

GREAT STAIRWAY

Mind where you step, Maggie. These stairs are tricky, like everything else round this place. The wood's been scalloped by thousands of boots and slippers. Slave brogans and moccasins, too. People come from all over to gawk at Charles Willson Peale's pile of dead animals. "Great School of Nature!" he called his museum. Boastful old man.

Here, you take the lantern, and I'll lead the way. Think you're too growed up to be skeered? Yes, I know you're eleven going on twelve, but I've seen square-shouldered men get mighty nervous up here. Look all pasty-face when they spy the tattooed human head and the black bugs puked up from a woman's stomach. A few say these grand rooms are a chamber of horrors.

I'll tell you why we're here in the gloom of evening, with only a shaving of moon to warm us, but first you'll need to catch your breath. Let's take a rest by this tall window.

Charles Willson Peale is kivered in muslin sheets tonight. Dead of pneumonia at eighty-six, though he bragged he'd see one hundred and twenty, maybe one-fifty years of age. That old Peale, he had a remedy for every sickness. I once saw him run up a hill with his mouth open, thinking he could cure a cold.

He'd been in fine health till lately, it's true. Courting women, playing with live rattlesnakes, making porcelain teeth, almost to the end. Some folks called him a great scientist and artist. Others said he was a cheap showman. Either way, looks like Death had more tricks than Mister Charley Peale.

Last year Charley wrote out the events of his lifetime. He titled it "The Life of Charles Willson Peale." I suspect a few smelly fish got left out of the story, specially the part about his oldest boy, Raphaelle, and how he lived a life of torment. Now that Rafe is gone someone needs to speak of things as they were for true. To untangle the chains that fastened Peale and Raphaelle to each other and me to them.

No, not chains of iron, Mag. There's other kinds of bondage. One is long words on fancy paper that say a white person can own a black one. T'other plays peekaboo at the back of the mind, so's a fellow hardly knows it's there. It lives on trust and longs to please when no pleasing will do. Twenty-three years ago, I wrestled free of both, but Raphaelle, he never learned to be his own man.

I think you're old enough to hear the tale, Maggie girl. Besides, I got no one else to hear me out, not since your pretty Irish mama passed over last year.

So quieten down and follow me up the stairs. The Museum is where it all began—my life with Charley Peale and the hard choices I made to get free. I aim to shed you every dark secret this place has to tell.

First Landing

Now then. A fellow can't ride the front of the horse without sitting on the rear. I got to start with Peale himself, else you won't understand the poison to come.

You got bugs in your shift, girl? Quit the squirming and look at this portrait on the window ledge. That's Peale in 1767 at age twenty-six, long before he kept slaves. Thin-visaged young fellow, wasn't he? Had a soft, sad look about his mouth. He was wounded as a boy, Ma said. No, not shot by a blunderbuss, or pierced with a blade. Young Charley Peale was hurt by shame.

Ma told me all about it one evening, when I was a little snipper. It was way past dark, and I was hoping to put off sleep time long as I could.

"Tell me a story, Ma," I begged. "Tell about Mr. Peale and how we came to live with him." To me, the master was a powerful smart man. Had him a mighty head, filled with ideas from books he kept in the parlor upstairs.

"It's too late for talk, Moses," Pa said. He was

PART I: ENTER

sharpening his barlow knife at the kitchen table. "Lucy's had her hands in the laundry tub all day."

"I don't mind," Ma said. "If Moses is so fond of Peale, it's time he should hear all about him. Bring my tin cup, boy."

She settled down on her bench by the fire. Your granny liked to tell stories, Mag, specially if she had her pipe and a cup of hard cider to ease the words along. And when she hitched her skirt between her legs and took a hearty swig, I figured I was in for a good long listen. Well, girl, I never thought of it that way—yes, our family has produced some great talkers. Some smarty young folks, too, I believe.

"I've picked up right many crumbs about Peale's family history," Ma started, "as it's good for slaves to learn anything they can about the master. Keeps things even. And I know for a fact that scandal has chased Peale his whole life.

"Some he can't help. Like his daddy being a criminal. Charles Wilson Peale, Sr. was born and raised in England. Had rich relatives and called himself a fine gentleman, though he stole from his employers. Before the law could swing him for the crime, he escaped to America in 1737. And that brings me to the second claw of the thing."

Ma took another sip. "Once he moves to Maryland, you see, he meets a woman. Marries her in 1741, but only when she's three months gone with their first son, Charles."

"A mongrel child," Pa said quietly from the

5

table. He added more oil to the whetstone and pushed the knife across. Blade said, *scritch-et, scritch-et*. Ma nodded and packed the bowl of her pipe.

"After fathering four more babes, Peale senior dies in 1750. With no money to speak of, Peale's mama has to bind out her eldest to a master saddle maker name of Nathan Waters. For seven years, young Charley toils every day but Sunday, sunrise to candlelighting. It must have been hard for him, knowing his daddy had left family money back in England."

Ma was getting sleepy, and so was I. I pulled my stool up to the bench, and she let me make a pillow of her soft belly. Her voice rolled on slow as mud.

"In 1760, when the apprenticeship is over, Charley Peale opens his own saddletree shop in Annapolis, Maryland. He fixes watches, larns silversmithing, teaches himself to paint signs and portraits. That's why he's as neat-a-hand as you'll ever see with tools, Moses. And how come he believes he can make anything work to suit him."

"Specially people," said Pa, "and we can vouch for that."

Ma sighed heavy but kept on.

"At age twenty-one Charley Peale meets our mistress, the small pale Rachel. She's but fourteen when he proposes. He gives her one hour to make up her mind, then stares at his watch, waiting for her to say yes."

"That's Peale, all right," Pa commented, "and bossy, still."

"But after he marries in 1762, Charles Peale brings disgrace on himself. He goes nine hundred pounds into debt. When the sheriff comes for him, he runs away, just like Peale senior. Charley is luckier than his Pa, though. Some rich folks send him out to London, England, to study about art. After three years he comes back to Annapolis and paints over one hundred portraits of rich people."

As Ma rubbed my head, a faraway sound crept into her voice. I watched the cup dangle from her hand as she talked, waiting for it to fall and clatter to the floor.

"Fellow makes himself a slew of money, don't you know, and roams over the Maryland countryside in a choice two-wheeled sulky. The portraits save Peale from scandal, but this doesn't satisfy him. Round that time, he tells a lie with his last name. Adds an extra *l* to Wilson."

"As if to separate himself from the shame of his birth," Pa put in. "Twas a small falsity, but a lie can grow like mold on bread, and don't you forget it, son."

Fingers of firelight crawled across the stone walls. Ma was silent. When I raised up to hear the rest of the story, her eyes were closed.

"Lucy, Lucy," Pa said softly. He caught the cup as it slipped from her hand, then pointed silently to my pallet on the floor.

"But Pa, how did we end up with Peale?" I

curled up under the blanket. Didn't seem fair. I'd heard a great chunk of grown-up words, yet no answer to my question.

"Time for sleep, boy," he whispered. "Your ma and I have chores to do at dawn."

Hard work and hard cider ended the story that evening, but don't worry, Mag, you'll hear the end of the tale, if I have to talk all night. No call to roll those eyeballs—you need to know the workings of the slaveholder's mind, what with Philadelphia's freed coloreds pinched into alleys and the almshouse packed with them that's out of work.

By and by, I learned more about Peale. Kept my ears open, the sneaky way that children do. Hand me my cane, and we'll go in the ticket office where there's less of a draft. I'll tell you about Peale's young ones and what he liked to call his "family" of slaves.

TICKET OFFICE

By 1772, Rachel had born four children. All perished in their babyhood. No, I don't know how they died—smallpox, perhaps.

Oftentimes fresh-born babes aren't strong enough for this rough world. Like your sister, Phoebe, who's resting in Strangers' Burial Ground. She would have turned eighteen last fall, had she lived through her infant fever. That being why I give thanks for my Maggie every Sunday at Bethel Church.

I'm sorry you grew up without a sister, too, but we have each other, don't we? You're a pea in my shoe sometimes, though a comfort in my old age, I admit. Knot your shawl a little tighter, girl, your chompers are shaking like dice. It's cold in this museum—must be a nor'easter blowing up the Delaware River.

In 1774, Peale came by his first slaves. He painted portraits of a rich Maryland couple, then traded them for Ma and Pa. Pa was named Scarborough, after the wife's maiden name, and Ma went by Lucy.

Peale called them his kitchen family. The kitchen part was true enough. Peale seated his slave quarters in the basement kitchen of the Annapolis house. Ma and Pa ate their meals down there and slept on a bed tick behind a curtain. Like the second *l* in his name, the family part was one more falsehood. I think holding slaves helped Peale play a pretend game in his mind. Let him make-believe he was high society instead of a lowly handyman. Helped him push away his own shame.

That same year, Rachel and Peale had Raphaelle, their first child to live past suckling time. Ma said Peale fussed over Raphaelle something fierce. Sewed fur caps for his little baby head. Mixed medicine to purge his bowels and held his head while he cast up his accounts.

So you see, Mag, Peale tethered Rafe to him from the start. Only trouble was, Rafe liked to jerk the rope. By the time Rafe was knee high, Ma claimed, he was a coddled child, indulged by Rachel and overprotected by Peale. Ma had her own thoughts on raising young ones. "You don't plant onions and get daffodils," she used to say.

This was two years before my time, a'course. I was born in 1776—the beginning of a hard time for Peale's family and slaves. Specially Ma, who was carrying me inside her.

In January '76, Peale moved his household from Annapolis here to Philadelphia. He was thinking there'd be more portraits to paint and more blast to fill his pockets. Blast? Peale's word for money, girl. Some saying he picked up in Maryland. Always trying to talk like the prissy plantation folks, Pa complained.

But in '76, the colonists were starting a rebellion against English rule. That's because England's crazy old King George believed he was a lion in the jungle. Thought he could bully the American colonies.

Now a bossy person hates a boss. Since Peale despised King George, he agreed to head up one of the militias from Philadelphia. He led the company through hellish battles against English troops in New Jersey. Cooked breakfast for his men and even made moccasins for their bloodied feet. He took care of those in his charge, I'll give you that.

But at the same time his family always came first. When British cannons roared near Philadelphia, Captain Peale left his men in the field. Rode powerful hard back to the city and wagoned his family to a safe place out in the country.

Being Peale's slaves, Ma and Pa had to follow along, so I spent a good part of my early baby days in a stage, rolling from one farmhouse to another. Ma, she always blamed my boyhood wildness on those uneasy months.

"Moses," she used to say, "the corduroy roads must have shook up your brains." Quit your cackling, Maggie, my cane's got a mighty long reach.

By '79, Peale was sick of soldiering. Tired of politicking, too, as none of the ump-de-umps in the Continental Congress could agree on much. The

Quaker delegates, they got pretty contentious over slavery.

"How can colonists keep black people in bondage," some of them stewed, "when the colonies are fighting a war for freedom?"

Don't look so bored with all this talk of slavery, Mag. You think freedom is free because you've always had it. Now listen up. This part's important.

In 1780, the Assemblymen passed what they called a manumission law. Said slaves born after that year must be freed at age twenty-eight. Peale was a delegate and voted with the "ayes," but it cost him nothing. He knew everybody in his kitchen family was born before 1780. According to the new ruling, he could hold us in slavery till we died.

"We got our hopes up high when the law passed," Pa remembered one time. "In keeping with the revolutionary spirit blowing through the city, some whites in Philadelphia were freeing their slaves, even ones born before 1780."

But Peale couldn't get past the need to have someone to wait on him, Pa said, so no one in the kitchen walked free that year.

TICKET COUNTER

You tired of standing, girl? Let's have us a sit-down at the counter here. First, hand me that painting of a house hanging on the side wall. The little oil sketch next to the cash drawer. And supposing you keep your mitts off that drawer. Nothing in it anyway. As you'll soon see, Charley spent every penny he had and was always looking to make more.

In August 1780, Peale bought this two-and-a-half-story building at the corner of Lombard and Third Streets. Moved his whole brood in, putting us slaves down in the kitchen, a'course, and commenced to paint miniatures on the second floor. Face pictures, he called them. Little oval portraits, no bigger than the palm of your hand. Quick to paint and a good way to keep Peale in blast.

The house in the sketch was the first of three homes for Peale's Museum. And it was the first home of my remembering. Twas a handsome brick place, tall up off the ground. Lombardy poplars round the front and glass-paned windows sparkling from all three floors.

Three more little Peales had arrived by then. Their daddy clapped the names of famous European artists on them, just like he did Raphaelle. Titian was the newborn son. Rembrandt, he was only two but already willful as a weed. Russet-headed Angelica was five and her daddy's rare flower.

Raphaelle was the oldest at six, a funny rascal, with long bangs and prankish eyes. After we settled down on Lombard, he was my fast friend, least till time and betrayal unraveled us apart like a frayed rope. Hand me your neckerchief, Maggie girl, I b'lieve these dusty rooms have given me a watery eye.

Peggy Durgan, Peale's nursemaid from childhood, helped Rachel with her babies. Being of a right good age, she had a toothless smile with sucked-up lips. Peggy looked like a prune, but she was a peaceable woman with kindly eyes.

Rachel got sorta snippy with us slaves. "Impudent baggage!" she hollered when Ma didn't step fast enough for her. I know it's hard for you to believe, Mag, as I've made sure no one talks that way to you.

But Peggy, she never made fuss or racket, and when Peale wasn't looking, she spoiled Rafe something awful. Called him her dear young fellow and always took his side, even when he was dead wrong.

Specially during the great battle of the bread. Peale's young ones loved Ma's crusty wheat bread the way Irish love taters. If they ate up the day's loaves by supper time, Rachel sent Angelica to the bakery two doors down for extra.

One evening, just when I had brought up a pitcher of milk, Rafe bit into the coarse baker's bread.

"This tastes like stable straw," he grumbled, spitting it into his linen napkin. I was amazed, as Pa would have jumped all over me had I done that downstairs.

"Raphaelle, I'll not tolerate a whim," Peale said, his voice hard as a black walnut. "You'll eat baker's bread from now on. You and the entire family."

"Charles, perhaps you are too hard on the children," Rachel said. Peale raised his eyebrows.

"A wife should follow her husband in these matters," he replied.

Rachel had nothing else to say. Peale's wife liked to rattle her house keys and order us slaves about, but she was a yessir, yessir woman round him. Angelica wept for real, more over the fighting than anything else, as she was a gentle girl. Rembrandt wailed dry crocodile tears, while Raphaelle's head hung low, regret smeared across his face like Ma's 'simmon jam.

Then Rafe winked at me, and I winked back, happy to be part of his private jest. Peale's sermons were just a trifling speck of fly dirt to Rafe, leastways when he was a little boy.

The war of wills twixt Peale and Raphaelle had begun. Seemed like Peale would win out at first. The family ate sour baker's bread every meal for the next two weeks. Ran up a twenty-pound bill at the bakery, I b'lieve.

Meantime, Peggy Durgan took pity on her Rafe. She slipped down to the kitchen and baked sweet knickknacks for him, though Ma didn't think too much of somebody messing up her copper kittles and pans.

Rafe and I had played together since our bare-bottom baby days, but the battle of the bread marked the start of a partnership in crime. Every day we sneaked out to the weeping willow in the backyard to gorge on currant cake or apple tart. One morning Peale caught us under the tree, sugar beards on our chins and the evidence in our hands.

"Moses, you go straight to the kitchen," he ordered. As I hot-tailed it across the yard, I overheard my friend get a good scolding.

"You're a pettish child, Raphaelle," preached Peale.

"I know, sir," Rafe replied. He sounded sorry as could be, but I suspected his mouth was playing hidey-smile. Neither of us got a big whooping, though Ma smacked the backs of my legs when she larnt of it.

Truth is, Peale wasn't as hard-boiled on us as some. A good many slaveholders make free with the whip, Mag. Give their slaves more stripes than they got teeth in their head. Like Pa's old master back in Maryland, what left some ridges on Pa's back. The whoopings made him into a silent, cautious man, Ma said. Yes, I saw the scars many a'time. Pa's back looked as wrinkled as the skin on cold gravy.

No . . . Peale claimed to be right fond of us downstairs folks. "You and your parents are my family within a family," he told me when I was a little tyke. It's one of my earliest memories—I think because the words gave me a safe feeling, like I belonged somewhere. And a child doesn't notice that some folks seem to belong in beds at night and some on pallets on the kitchen floor.

Charley even had us all baptized across the street at Saint Peter's, where he held a fancy high-back box pew. Ma still carried a lucky bone charm in a bag round her neck, but she took to praying, too. Most Sabbath days she attended the service, and one Sunday she came home foretelling the doom of Peale's soul.

"You should have come today," Ma told Pa. "White preacher said something interesting." She tied on her apron and proceeded to chop carrots for the Peales' midday meal. "He claims a Christian can't keep fellow Christians in slavery, only heathens."

Pa was polishing Rachel's silver spoons.

"Aren't we Christians," he asked as he rubbed, "now that we been baptized?"

Ma waved the cleaver in the air, and Pa ducked. "Peale wouldn't let us go for heaven or hell. Who would wash his laundry? Clean the stable? Tote the coal? Appears like he's traveling a turnpike to damnation. Come Judgment Day, he'll pay the toll!"

I was just a believing boy. Old enough to pick up chips to start the fire, but too young to ask why I had to eat in the kitchen. None of Ma's ranting made sense. To my four-year-old mind, I *was* one of Peale's kin and Raphaelle was my brother. For a mighty long while, he was.

Up the
Tower Steps

As time passed, Rafe and I did everything together, though he was two years older. He was the big hand on the clock, I was the little one following behind. Take the night folks burned Major General Benedict Arnold.

No, girl, they didn't burn Arnold straight out, of course, just a dummy of him. You can see it plain in a picture tacked to the tower staircase wall—Peale framed the drawing after it appeared in the *Sunday Dispatch*. We'll go through the lecture room and head to the top of the tower, Mag, then work our way down. Easy now, these steps are steep. Your knees might be achy from the last climb—use the banister if you feel a need.

It happened in late September 1780, around two months after we moved into the house on Lombard. When Arnold betrayed his countrymen by letting out a military secret to the British, Peale and some army officers planned a revengeful parade.

As Rafe and I looked on, Peale made a two-faced effigy of Arnold in the backyard. We were talky little monkeys, full of chatter.

"How did you do that, Father?"

"Why'd you do this, Mr. Peale?"

Charley got tired of the questions, a situation I do now fully understand. He finally let us stuff old Arnold with straw, and when he made a dummy of a devil, he let us stick horns in its head.

Peale set the devil behind Arnold, so's it looked like he was speaking into the spy's ear. Next he built a stage on a cart and placed the whole scene upon it.

"Raphaelle, during the parade I want you to lie under the stage and pull the cord that turns Arnold's head."

"Let me help, Mr. Peale," I begged. I grabbed holt of his leg. "I'm little enough!"

"Surely your parents will need you in the kitchen," Peale replied as he tied a pitchfork into the devil's right hand.

Tears crawled round the front of my eyeballs, though I never let one drop fall. I see now Charley thought it was only sensible to choose his child, not a slave. Yet I believed I was like a son to him, you understand, and he was like a god to me.

"Can't you let us both go, Father?" Rafe asked. Peale settled it quick enough.

"The space is sufficient for only one."

Rafe wiggled under the stage, and as soon as Charley turned his back, my friend . . . my brother . . . signaled to me.

"Psst! Moze!"

He scooted his long, skinny legs over to make room for my shorter ones. I climbed in and off we rode, Peale leading the horse and Rafe and me in the back, cozy as two worms under a rock.

The procession began about four o'clock that afternoon. Thousands of folks lined the streets, while two boys circled the cart playing "Rogues March" on fife and drum. Militiamen stepped smart on either side, candles blazing from the barrels of their muskets. In the blackness under the stage, Rafe and I smothered laughs and took turns pulling the cord. Every time we gave a tug, the crowds roared with hate.

"Burn the traitor!"

"Send him to Hades where he belongs!"

After dark, the soldiers lit a bonfire. Directly before they hurled the effigy into the flames, Peale reached in to pluck Rafe from the cart. When he spied four feet instead of two, he let out a surprised holler.

"What foolishness is this?" he cried, then jerked Rafe and me out. We still had a case of the giggles, and that made Charley even madder, though we straightened up right quick, I'll tell you that! Peale cotched us up by the hands and plopped us on the ground.

"Stay put," he ordered, "and keep away from the flames!"

After the fire, folks heaped compliments upon him for his clever piece of theater. He was pretty full of himself, yet he didn't forget to give Rafe a harsh lecture later. That was the thing. When Rafe got attention from Charley, it was generally for the wrong reason. Ma? Well, a'course, she set a switch to my legs when I got back to the kitchen.

Ah, Maggie, what a time Rafe and I had! You might think all we shared was trouble. We found us some fun, too, least till Rafe turned eight and started going to the Madam's School.

Seemed like the broad Delaware River was made for our particular amusement. It was only three blocks over, and on the coldest winter days, we went ice-skating every chance we got. Glided smooth and pretty on our gutter skates, like dancers in a cotillion. Rafe loved to fall down and sail on his behind across the ice. Liked that part better than skating, I b'lieve.

"Watch this, Moze!" he'd call, trying a backward jump. And down he'd slide, a wild holler percolating up from his toenails. Rafe usually stripped the fanny threads off his britches when we went skating. Peggy Durgan patched them back together a heap o' times, though she never let on to Rafe's folks.

In spring, we walked to Mullen's Dock at the foot of Walnut Street. It was the best spot for swimming. Had a fine gravel bottom so's we could wade out to our knees and yell "whoo-ee" when the cold water inched up to our privates.

Come warm weather, we went clear out Third Street till it turned into meadow. The field sloped down to Peg's Run, a creek where we fished for bullheads when the freshet came. If the creek ran low, we dug for pirate's gold on the bank with two of Pa's carved wooden spoons.

One June day, Rafe painted a pebble with his Daddy's gold watercolor paint and hid it in his pocket. Planted it in the bank when I wasn't looking. When my spoon clunked upon the rock, I hopped round like Peale's cockatoo.

"Rafe, looky here!" I yelled. "Gold! This will buy us nine pence of candy at the confectionary shop!"

"At least that much, Moze! And a set of marbles, too. Maybe a fashion doll for Angelica. Or a pony for each of us!"

Then I saw Rafe snickering behind his hand. Before long, my fingers turned shiny bright, and the piece of gold changed back to a plain gray rock. Thinking about the lost confection, I was mighty vexed with him, but that evening I got my revenge. Waited till he was sitting pretty on his throne in the outhouse, halfway to stark mother nekkid. Then I flung the door open, took aim, and dashed the varmint with cold water.

Don't look so surprised, Maggie. It's best you know what nonsense young fellows get themselves into, in case you have some of your own. Anyhow, I never could stay mad at Rafe for long. He had a way of tricking me so I'd laugh at myself and still feel good about it.

Rembrandt was a different situation altogether. In those years he was too small to play with us, him a toddling baby and all. He wobbled after Rafe and me on fat cream puff legs, wailing to take him with us. We just walked faster, leaving him to cry in Peggy Durgan's skirts.

Maybe we should have brought him along. While we searched for great adventure, Rembrandt stayed at home with Peale, getting sour as bad milk. I never figured out why Peale put such a special store by Rembrandt. Used to call him his talented one, and goodness knows, Charley wanted his own to make him proud.

But Peale never could abide his oldest child's mischief. Somewheres along the way, Rafe became the prodigal son. That's the boy in the Bible who shames his Pa.

BELL CHAMBER

Lordy, what a climb this is! Don't stump your toe on the bell—the Independence Bell folks call it, but that's a two-thousand-pound lie. On account of the words round the top: "Proclaim liberty throughout all the land, unto all the inhabitants thereof." Yes, I know my Bible as well as you, Missy. Leviticus— the Third Book of Moses in the Old Testament. No, not quite *all* the inhabitants of the land, no ma'am. Maybe that's why the bell cracked the first time they rang it.

Take a look at the drawing tacked to the rafters, Mag. Peale stuck it up here over forty years ago. Careful, now, the paper is rubbed thin along the folds. Here, you hold it, since my fingers are gouty of late. Besides, I don't need a picture to recall my first hint that Peale was no god—just an ordinary greedy man.

In 1783 England and the United States signed the Treaty of Paris. The Revolutionary War was over, and Congress asked Peale to build a display to mark the occasion. Peale couldn't pass up a chance to show off. This time, though, it cost him a considerable amount of money. Almost cost him his life, too.

For two months Charley labored like a beaver building a lodge. In the drawing you can see the forty-foot wooden timbers his helpers set up. The timbers served as columns. Held up three arches that stretched clear across Market Street, the middle one being twenty feet high.

Peale made thirteen paintings on window-shade cloth, one for each of the colonies. He plastered them all over the huge frame, leaving room for a candle behind each one. Strewn across the top were paper figures of Justice, Prudence, Temperance, and Fortitude. Peace was in the middle. You'll notice, Maggie, that Freedom was nowhere in sight.

For weeks, people talked about Peale's Triumphal Arch and how twould be lit up in late January, 1784. Since Rachel was expecting, she was too skeered to go in the crowded streets. But being that Rafe was nine, Peale thought he was old enough to see the display. Charley's younger brother, James, lived nearby, and he agreed to take Raphaelle to the roof of General George Washington's mansion.

On the morning of January twenty-second, Ma sent me to fetch water from the corner pump. Rafe traipsed along and got to pleading with me.

"Moze, come with us tonight. You and I can drop snowballs down into the crowd. We'll pack them soft and loose, so people won't know what hit them."

"You heard your father yesterday!" I replied. "He said, 'Any boys who disturb the peace by throwing squibs or crackers will be sent to the workhouse!'"

Rafe chuckled. "Firecrackers, yes, but not snowballs. Anyway, Father's threat is only for street urchins, not his own boys."

The words heartened me, so I spoke to Ma and Pa about it mid-morning, leaving out the snowball part, of course. Pa was against it.

"Son, you best stay home and help me split wood," he said. "That Raphaelle is a troublesome child. When you don't find mischief on your own, he finds it for you."

Though I suspected Pa was right, I whined a bit till he caved in. I needn't have worried about the workhouse, because when Rafe and I reached the roof that evening, we forgot all about snowballs. We were too taken with the sight below us. Bands playing. Thousands of people milling about the streets, wrapped warm in furs and knitten wool. All this because of Peale! I felt proud to be part of his family. Pleased I lived in the household of such a clever and powerful man.

At twilight, soldiers lit over one thousand lamps placed upon the framed arches. What a grand sight it seemed, those golden lights against a tarnished tin sky. Then Peale climbed the middle arch to light the lamp behind Peace. This would be his signal for soldiers to ignite seven hundred rockets below.

Just as he commenced to light the lamp, a stray firecracker exploded. Sparks winged over the arches and landed on a parcel of rockets. Those firecrackers exploded like popped Indian corn, and in seconds, Peale's Triumphal Arch was ablaze.

Rafe and I huddled together on the windy roof, pretty much frightened by the screams of terror all around. His uncle James rushed us through the house, down the steps, and into the panicky streets. It's a wonder we didn't get lost or stomped, with folks running this way and that, but James held our hands, and for once we stayed out of trouble. Not one giggle passed between us, no ma'am.

What happened to Peale? Hold on, now, first things first. Rachel stuck to Raphaelle like glue when we came in the door. The last I saw of my friend that night, he could hardly breathe for his mama's kisses.

I ran straight to the kitchen, where Ma was setting by the fire with her cider. Your granny was a low, chunky-looking woman, Maggie, like an ironwood tree that bends with the wind. That night, though, it appeared like she was starting to crack.

"Moses!" she hollered when she spied me, her voice trembling. She threw her apron over her head and burst into tears.

Pa led me to the warm hearth, as I was still shaking with excitement. Well, all right, Maggie, have it your way. I reckon I was afraid some, too.

"We thought you'd been burned," Pa said. "Scorched like Mister Peale."

"Mister Peale? Burned?" Peale, smoking like a green log—it was an outlandish thought. Not Peale, the master, the man who was more'n a man.

"When the arch caught," Pa said, "Peale jumped down to a post, then lost his holt when a packet of rockets burst below. He fell straight into the flames."

I squinched my face while Ma forced everlasting boneset tea down my throat. "Pa," I whispered, "did he die?"

"Don't look so worried. Peale ran hard as he could stave into a nearby house. Doused his clothes with water, jumped in a passing sleigh, and begged a ride. Got home quick, about a half hour ago."

"Old Charley was a sight when he stumbled in the house," Ma said. "Two ribs cracked, and his pale locks black as the hairs on one of my roasted chickens."

"The man was hurting," said Pa. "Looked like a flag. A little white skin here and there, but mostly raw red burns and blue bruises. Your ma and I, we wanted to head out and find you right off."

"But Charley had his own needs," Ma said.

"As Rachel helped Peale up the stairs," Pa continued, "he called down a slew of orders. 'Lucy, prepare a poultice of butter and ash. Scarborough, mix a pitcher of lead water. And bring clean rags!'

"We did that," Pa went on, "and made ready to leave. Then Rachel told us to wait in the kitchen."

"Said she might need us again," Ma said, her eyes still wet.

Pa was troubled, I could tell, since it was rare for him to string so many words together at one time. No, I'm not much like him in that way, Mag. And if you don't leave off the insults, your tongue's going to feel like it's been in an accident.

Looking back on that night, I see things more clearly. Ma and Pa, worried about me and nothing to do except wait as they were ordered and hope I was alive. But me, I was still curious about Peale. If he was so powerful, how could all his plans fall apart so fast? How bad was he hurt?

Charley was piled up in bed for the next three weeks. Every morning I took breakfast to him, and one day I quietly entered his chamber to pick up the tray. Heard him ranting to no one in particular.

"Ingratitude…must beg for recompense…portraits… lost income… "

Ma quizzed me when I returned to the kitchen. "How is our hero this morning, Moses?"

I set the tray on the table and picked at Peale's leftover toast. "Talking something about recompense, Ma. What is that?"

She snorted. "It's money, Moses. Something Charley never seems to have."

"You'd think Peale would be happy to be alive," Pa remarked. "Lots of folks got burned in the inferno. A couple of fellows died, including the poor sergeant in charge of the rockets."

"A lot more'n Peale's ribs were hurt that night.

When his precious arch burned, his pride got singed, too," Ma said. "On top of that, he's bitter. Pained over portrait money he lost while working on the arch."

"And every time he runs out of blast," Pa said, "our chances of going free get thinner than a ha' cent."

Their talk was a puzzlement to me, a sprout of seven. Why would Peale be bitter? Wasn't he a great and fair man, called upon by his country? And what of us going free? He liked to think of us as family, and he hated the thought of having a master. I'd heard him talk about his years of working for Nathan Waters. How the morning his bound-time was over was the happiest moment of his life.

Sometimes the truth is an itching in the middle of your back, Maggie. You can't reach it too easy or for very long. But slowly, as I grew older, I began to see that slavery wasn't about being part of a family. That freedom wasn't about being fair. It was all about money, plain and simple. As long as Peale was bound to money, we were bound to him.

CLOSET

How you holding up? I've not heard a question in a while. Yes, the air here in the bell chamber is chilly, and the wind is picking up. Warm your hands on the lantern glass, why don't you?

Peale's burns healed directly, and Rachel had another son in May 1784. Rubens was a sickly little babe. He brought out Rachel's sweeter side, something the kitchen family didn't see too often, though she was kind enough to her own brood upstairs.

"Rubens, you're so small," she'd coo to the bundle in the cradle, "I could put you in a silver mug and close the lid." Used to make me gag to hear her singsong talk, as she never spoke that nice to me.

Well, with a fifth child springing up quick like that, Peale couldn't paint fast enough. He cast about for a new money-making plan and came up with the idea for a moving pictures show. It was then I first understood that Rafe and I warn't brothers, after all.

Peale drove himself hard as a coach-and-four, thinking of ideas for the show. For more'n a year, he roamed the house while his family was asleep. Looked kinda vagueish in his nightshirt, like a spirit from one of the Africky stories Ma told round the hearth. I was none too pleased when he called upon me to tend him on his nightly rambles.

"Moses!" he shouted down the basement steps one cold midnight, the nightshirt bunched round his knobby knees and a red flannel cap slipping off his pate. "Come stoke the fireplace in the painting room!"

"Moses! Bring a bottle of cider straightaway!"

Hadn't been for Pa, I'd a'slept through the racket. "You hear Mister Peale hollering for you, son?" Pa called, his voice sleepy-thick behind the curtain.

"Yessir," came my wearisome reply. Up the stairs I climbed, head foggy with dreams and feet bare as a lamb's rump.

On long nights like these, old Peale mumbled constant about which scenes to paint and how to light them. And after a year of hearing about it, I couldn't wait to see the show come to life.

Look there in the closet, Mag. You'll find six pictures Charley painted. Most are half rotten now. Watch yourself, girl! Don't want those splintery old frames to tear your linsey skirt. That one on top is a palace. Peale used it as the backdrop for a cloudy sky that poured rain, then turned into a rainbow. And the one underneath is a sunrise scene.

The day before *The Moving Pictures with Changeable Effects* opened in May of 1785, Rafe rushed down the kitchen steps. I was chucking wood in the bake oven.

"Come quickly, Moses. Father is teaching us all manner of tricks!"

I looked at Pa. I knew what he was thinking. That trouble would follow me if I followed my friend.

"I got chores to do, Rafe."

"Moze, I won't enjoy it half as much without you." He gave me a secret grin. "And I am certain Father will have need of your assistance." That sly Rafe knew Pa would agree, as a slave can't refuse to help the master.

Pa sighed. "If Mr. Peale needs Moses, he might as well go now as later."

Rafe and I raced up the stairs two at a time. What a play-party it was in the painting room! We arrived just as Charley handed Titian a sheet of copper.

"Titian," he said, "you shall be in charge of sound effects." Peale closed his big hand over the boy's tiny paw and gave him an encouraging smile. "To make thunder, you must shake it hard."

Then he gave the little fellow a pan of peas. Told him how to rattle the pan so's it sounded like a hard rain. Titian enjoyed the job, I could tell, as it thundered and poured in the house for the rest of the day.

Angelica was ten, no bigger'n a bar of soap, but

quick-fingered. "Angelica, my rose," Peale announced with a flourish, "you will operate the lights!"

Charley put a stack of colored stained glass on a table near the stage. "Hold these one at a time in front of the Argand lamp," he instructed. "As you change the glass, a different color will shine upon the painted scenes."

Rembrandt? He worked Peale's three barrel organs that played some thirty tunes. Sniveled about his sore arms after a few minutes of practice, as those stiff cranks had to go on the fly.

Finally Peale turned to Rafe. "You are the tallest and will have the biggest task," Charley said. "I will instruct you in my system of pulleys. They will move the curtains and screens that keep each scene hidden from view."

"Let Moses assist me, Father," Rafe begged. "We shan't make trouble, we promise!"

"I'll do a good job, Mr. Peale," I said, "I swear to God." Doing anything with Rafe would be more sport than work, and I ached to be a part of the excitement. But grown-ups don't always heed young'uns like they should, and I'll thank you not to smirk, Mag.

"Swearing is an unpleasant custom, generally," Charley replied. "And Raphaelle should assume some responsibility on his own."

That Rembrandt, he was watching us close, him with his jack-o'-lantern eyes.

"Let Moses turn the organ cranks, Father," he

35

said, rubbing his aching arm. "*I* should help Raphaelle, since *I* am his brother."

"Yes, but Moses is my friend," Rafe shot back.

It was plain that Rafe favored me over his own kin. Peale didn't like the smell of that at all. He looked sharply at the two and slammed the subject shut.

"Raphaelle will work the curtains," he said. "Rembrandt will crank the organs, and Moses will return to the kitchen, where he has his own tasks to perform."

You're right, Mag. Peale could have let my friend have his way. No harm in it. But Charley was so used to ruling Rafe, he didn't know when to stop. And Rafe was let down some, yes. His chin so low, looked like it was having a get-together with his neck. Me? I was fired-up proper because suddenly I saw it clear as glass. Peale's kitchen family was useful enough in the middle of the night, but not good enough to work alongside his children! I stomped back downstairs, determined to see the moving pictures, no matter what.

Peale's debut was a success, I'll grant you. The next day, the painting room was packed with fifty ladies and gents. After the show began, I sneaked in, and it was an amazement to my nine-year-old eyes. The sounds, lights, and moving scenery all changing at once made Peale's illusions seem monstrous true. I liken it to a play with no actors, but a heap more exciting.

When the two-hour display ended, folks filed

past Peale, impressed with the rosy dawn and pink nightfall they'd seen upon the stage. Charley preened like one of his bug-eyed parrots.

"You can thank Rembrandt for the music," he said proudly, putting a hand atop his pox-of-a-son's head.

Yes, I guess you could say that, Mag. It appears by now Peale's sun did truly rise and set with Rembrandt. Even at seven, the boy was a smart one. Somehow he knew how to play upon Peale. To turn his daddy's head toward him. Meanwhile, Rafe stood nearby, fooling with his knee laces and waiting for the compliment that never came.

I'll tell you what's the truth, Rafe wasn't the only one to feel shunt aside. During 1785 and 1786, the two years Peale ran his show, I was squeezed out of my friend's life, piecemeal. Grew into manhood duties quick as I grew into homespun breeches.

While Rafe was helping with the show, I fed birds to the vipers Peale kept caged in the yard. I remember a great yearning to lift the cage door—to let the snakes slither away, since I was starting to feel trapped myself. Times when Rafe and I would skate and swim together were gone, as he grew into other things.

When Rafe left the house for dance lessons, I collected his soiled clothes and took them to Ma in the laundry. As Rafe learned French from a tutor in the small parlor, I polished his boots in the kitchen.

And a'course, I helped Pa with the everlasting burden of wood. If I never haul another stick of firewood, I will die a cheerful man. Lay off that frowning, girl. I know you have no affection for the job, but looky here. I'm fifty years old now. Seems some privileges ought to come with getting ageable. You might have to cart wood, but at least you're not struggling in the streets, like some children I know.

VENT

Let's perch a while on this floor beam by the bell, and I'll tell you what I mean. Feeling closed in? Well, stand by the vent so's you can peek out at the moon. It's shuttered tight, but I see a few loose slats.

Now, before you let fly with more complaints, I'll show you what your daddy's hard work has saved you from. It's stored in this box in the corner. Be careful of the cobwebs—they're catching in your hair.

Peale called this etching *The Accident in Lombard Street*. Twas part of a set he expected to sell, but he lost money as usual, since folks warn't willing to pay twenty-five cents for a crude picture with a silly rhyme:

> THE PYE FROM THE BAKE–HOUSE SHE
>   HAD BROUGHT
> BUT LET IT FALL FOR WANT OF THOUGHT
> AND LAUGHING SWEEPS COLLECT AROUND
> THE PYE THAT'S SCATTERED ON THE
>   GROUND.

The ACCIDENT in LOMBARD-STREET PHILAD.ª 1787

Here is the house on Lombard and the bakery two doors down. The girl? That's Angelica, weeping over the boughten pie she dropped on the cobbled street.

Those filthy fellows with soot bags are chimney sweeps, indentured children name of Israel, Benjamin, and Joe. They worked the houses round Lombard pretty regular. I used to listen for their cries in the morning.

> SWEEP FOR YOUR SOOT, HO,
> I AM THE MAN,
> THAT YOUR CHIMNEY WILL CLEAN
> IF ANYONE CAN,
> SWEEP, HO!

When we first moved to Lombard, the sweeps seemed free as cats to me, going about the streets at will. But Ma, she didn't let me rove with them much.

"You steer clear of them, Moses," she said. "They're a restless pack a'wolves and foul-smelling to boot." Soon as I heard their call, though, I slipped out the kitchen door before Ma could grab me, hoping for a game of chuckers by the curb.

Israel, he was the youngest at seven. Still a slave, but hired out by his master for a yearly fee of fifteen pounds. He kept sores on his knees from heisting his skinny body up thirty-foot chimneys.

Benjamin was a free child, nine years of age. Had him a rusty cough. His lungs were already rotten with soot, even with the floppy hat he pulled over his face while in the flues. Died early on, around twelve, I recall.

Joe could chuck a stone in a hole better'n any of the Peale boys, though his legs were twisty. Grown crooked from wedging himself in the chimneys. The tall boy on the right is Caesar, the head sweep and a runaway slave from the South. He handled the money end of things. Most of it landed in his pocket, I believe.

On the day of Angelica's accident, the boys had little else to laugh about, I'll tell you straight out. Hungry bellies sticking to their backs, most likely, and wishing they could grab scraps of pie before Peale's dog, Argus, lapped them up.

You've always lived in warm quarters in our two-story brick house on Sterling Alley, Mag. I've seen to that. Always had three meals a day. But there's plenty of black children in Philadelphia only halfway to free, like the boys in the picture. Apprenticed by a slave master or bound out by poor free parents till they're twenty-one. It was a common practice when I was a child. Still is.

Some children larn a trade like tinning or smithing, it's true, and by law how to read and write. This last is a boon to the slaves, as few are allowed to learn. But the only pay for free children is their freedom dues—a few sets of clothes to wear after they been thrown out on their own. Some are even sold back into slavery.

This wasn't the childhood I wished for you, girl. A miserable life of sweat with no hope for better. That being why I send you to the school on Gaskill Street each morning. It's my jubilation to watch your learning grow every day, like dollars in a bank. No call to look put out, Mag. You might think the texts are heavy, but book smarts will keep you free, and school is a choice I never had.

Ma and Pa didn't want a sweeper's life for me, either. So when Peale's conscience finally swatted him in the face about slavery, they were all torn up over the fate of their boy. One more flight of steps, and I'll tell you how it happened.

BELFRY

We're at the peak of the tower now. Take care—the steps are narrow, with three twists and turns. Remember to lower your head, since we won't be able to stand up straight under the slanted roof. The swooshing sound? Why, that's only the bats what call this cramped space home.

Peale had a high-up white friend, a doctor name of Benjamin Rush. Been knowing him a long time. Rush, he was neat-a-built man as ever was seen in Philadelphia and longways the colored people's best white friend.

Rush was none too satisfied with the slavery situation. One time he came to visit Peale, and Pa heard them talking backwards and forwards in the parlor. Rush going one way against the bondage of black people, Peale going t'other.

Charley must have listened, because early in 1786, he came down to the kitchen for a stiff-shouldered talk. Sat on Ma's bench by the fire and shifted his haunches an inch or so.

"Lucy and Scarborough," Peale said, folding

his hands and clearing his throat. "As soon as I am able, I will replace you with hired servants. At that time, it is my intention to give you your free papers and let you go. Unless you prefer to work for wages here," he added.

I wondered why Peale had not mentioned me. Ma lifted a pot off the fireplace hitch, then smoothed her apron. Pa put down the pewter plate he'd been scouring slow and hard. They looked at each other and said nothing. Knowing how Ma loved my legs, I kept still as a hare a'setting.

"I reckon we'll scratch for our own selves, Mr. Peale, but what of our Moses?" she asked. Her voice trembled like boiled custard. "Are you of a mind to free him, too? Or will you be binding him out?"

Indentured servitude! There's the devil that you don't know, and the devil that you do. I'd learned to read Peale's moods and puzzle out his ways. Figured I was better off with him than a new master. At least he wouldn't beat me, nor would I starve. And if I remained a slave in his house, he might let me go free in a year or so. I hooked my hopes to that shiny thought.

Peale strode over to the basement stairs. He climbed the first one as if it were a stage and spread one arm out. Commenced to give a grand-sounding speech.

"I have great plans for this house, Lucy," he said, his blue eyes swimming toward some far-off dream. "I hope to make it a glorious repository of natural curiosities, a museum of learning and science. It will be a fitting collection for our new country, and your son will have to play his part in it."

Then Peale's voice got silky, like he was handing Ma a gift.

"Moses will be freed on his twenty-eighth birthday." He gave her a satisfied smile. "Perhaps sooner, if he conducts himself with industry and perseverance."

Almost twenty more years of slavery! To a June Bug boy of nine, it seemed far off as Judgment Day. Peale's words made me feel awful bad and set me near to bawling.

About that time, Rafe came running down the steps, calling, "Lucy, can Moses come outside—"

He stopped short on the bottom step, like a squirrel caught with an acorn in his mouth.

Peale frowned. "Raphaelle, I am conducting private business. You should be in the parlor practicing your French."

When Rafe glanced at me, I blinked hard. Ashamed of the tears, you know.

"What has happened, Moze?" he asked.

Like Pa, Ma never back talked or loud talked the Peales to their faces. That night, though, she wheeled around and come off. "Your father intends to set us free, Raphaelle, but he will be keeping our boy." Ma flung out the words like she was throwing peelings to the pigs. "You'll still have your playmate. When you can find time between schooling and dancing, that is!"

As her voice rang off the cold walls, Rafe's face turned to mush. He knew then what I had learned during the moving pictures show. That our friendship might float along for a while, but as long as I was a slave, there was only one way it could go.

"Take care, Lucy," Peale warned. "I cannot allow you to speak with disrespect." Pa was quiet, though I figured he was tied in a knot. Thinking Peale might get angry enough to keep him and Ma, after all.

"Father, you mustn't do it," Rafe begged. "Let Moses go with his parents. It's only right—he is their son, as much as I am yours."

For Rafe's sake, I wished he would shut his gob and save himself. No, Rafe wouldn't get a whooping, Mag. Peale knew how to lay a sharper sting on his son. Shame, if properly seasoned, he liked to say, is a greater scourge than the birch. Charley would ignore Rafe for hours to come. Not pay him any more mind than a shadow, just to prove who was in charge.

"To the parlor," Peale said. "Immediately."

Rafe looked sorrowful at me and scuffed up the steps. I tuned up to cry for real and felt Pa's hands upon my shoulders. When Peale saw this, a cloud passed over his scrawny face. Maybe he felt a little sorry, now that Rafe had reminded him he was cleaving the kitchen family in two.

"Scarborough, you and Lucy may need some assistance in your new life," Peale said. He wiped both hands on his vest as if sweating shame.

"Although my funds are limited, I'll give you money to rent a place of your own. If need be, I'll help you secure employment, as well."

He started up the stairs. "And if circumstances warrant, you can come to me for a loan," he added. Peale tacked this last promise onto the end, like a stump-tail on a bulldog.

You never know where good is coming from, Mag, or bad. Though it didn't seem so that night, I had begun a long journey toward freeing myself. And set out upon the rocky road of deceit.

DOWN THE
TOWER STEPS

You seem a little jumpy, girl. No, the tower won't fall over. It's only the wind what makes it sway. We'll go down to the Marine Room, now. Have a rest and a bite of this pippin I been carrying in my pocket. The squealing sound? That's the rats— here, I'll swing the lantern to warn them we're coming through.

Peale gave Ma and Pa their free papers late in the winter of 1786, and one gray dawn they moved out of Lombard Street. Warn't going far. Just to a rackety shack up on Elbow Lane, where some colored families lived poor but free. Didn't have much to carry, neither. What little they owned fit inside a handbarrow built by Pa. They had plenty of plans, though.

Ma and I stood outside the kitchen door in the freezing rain while Pa loaded the cart. No, Mag, nary a Peale was in sight. Still heaped up in their plump warm beds, I expect.

"First thing to do is get shuck of my name," Pa said. He wedged a wool comfort under an ax handle.

"It never was mine to begin with. I'll answer only to John Williams from this day on!"

"And we'll get wedded in a church," Ma said, "as we had only a broomstick marriage back in Maryland. I know a colored preacher, a former slave name of Richard Allen. I've heard him speak at daytime meetings on the commons up the street. We'll ask him to marry us."

When they were finally ready to leave, seemed like the last minute of the world to me. That's a good way to put it, Mag. Saying good-bye is like pressing a wound. You think it will help the hurt, but it only makes it bleed more.

As Pa unlatched the gate between the stable and the house, Ma bussed my forehead. "Moses, you'll always be next to my heart," she said softly. "Watch those wild ways—you'll still be near the back of my hand."

Pa grew uncommonly quiet, even for him. He handed me a good-sized wooden lockbox he'd carved with a jackknife. It was five inches deep and ten inches long, about the size of Peale's tea caddy.

"Open it, son."

What a fine gift! I'd seen Pa spend long hours shaping the snake design that curved around the sides. When I turned the key and lifted the lid, I found a poplar whistle nestled in a scrap of red cloth.

"Now you'll always have a place to keep a secret," he said. I croaked out a thank-you, gave my folks one last squeeze, then held the gate open for them. As I watched them head out for a life of their own, I swore a swear—I vowed to please Peale as best I could. The words "industry and perseverance" jiggled in my head like a bunch of keys, and that morning I believed they would soon set me free.

The following week, Richard Allen agreed to marry Ma and Pa up at Saint George's, the Methodist church where free blacks went to service with whites. Peale said yes, I could go if it was on a Sunday, this being most slaves' day off.

Ma looked pretty that morning. She wore a sprigged muslin dress Peggy Durgan gave her, though it dragged a bit on the dirt floor of the church. Pa had a friend, a music man called Peter. After Preacher Allen declared Ma and Pa to be legal man and wife, we all headed back to Elbow Lane. Peter fiddled while we drank cider and cut the buck and pigeonwing. Had us a sure enough jollification that stayed with me for days.

I did worry some when Pa had trouble finding work. He hired himself out making barrels for a cooper. Then he was replaced by a white laborer and ended up at the docks. Unloaded indigo and molasses from the ships what put in there every day.

Ma took in laundry, like most of the colored women on Elbow Lane. With both Ma and Pa working, they made out all right and didn't need Peale's help at all. But within a few months, I had little time left to think about my kin. Seemed like I had a lot of my own matters to ponder at once.

First off, Peale did a flip-flop about holding slaves. Rachel delivered another girl, Sophy, in April, and old Charley needed more help with his nestful of babes. He couldn't pay a hired woman, so he traded some portraits for a slave named Philis.

Now this was a trick only Peale could pull. Handing two slaves their freedom, then finding one more. Lifted a shred of caul from my eyes, Maggie, I'll say that. When you get right down to it, Peale was a weak man, weak as water.

Yes, it was a relief to have a companion in the kitchen, I admit. I didn't relish sleeping alone down there, wrapped in blankets on the stone floor. Nothing but Pa's whistle under my pillow for company.

And Philis was the handsomest pretty lady I ever saw. Copper-complected, like you, girl. If I could've picked someone to be my big sister, I'd have picked her. She didn't make oyster soup as good as Ma, but she had a straight-up way that made me feel braver than I was.

That spring, Peale decided it was time for young Titian and Rembrandt to larn their letters. He taught the boys every day in the small parlor on the first floor. I hinged myself in the doorway, picking up crumbs of schooling when I could.

Peale noticed me lingering there one day. "Come in," he said, waving me inside. Charley was still feeling guilty, I'm sure of it. I took a few steps, feeling like a trespasser.

"Rembrandt, loan Moses one of your pencils."

From the looks of Rembrandt, you'd a'thought he had to loan me gold instead of lead. "But, Father..."

Peale interrupted him. "Titian, give Moses some of your foolscap." Titian handed me the scrap paper. "Now you can practice letters on your own, Moses," Peale said.

"In the kitchen," Rembrandt added.

I wonder if Peale would have been so generous if he'd known what he'd done. That reading would open a window and let his lies out. And I wonder— would I have chosen to learn what I know now?

But back then, I craved anything to keep from looking at the empty bench where Ma used to sit. Every night, I hunched over the kitchen table and copied capital letters from handbills.

Philis peeked over my shoulder one evening. "Those are pretty figures, Moses."

"They're not so good," I protested, but twixt you and me, Mag, she was right. I was more exacting with my curves and lines than ever Rembrandt was. It's not a boast, girl. Twas the truth!

Then Charley decided his children had to live up to their artist names. He learned them how to draw and how to paint face pictures. Gave them art books to teach them about line and color.

Rafe hated learning art from books. Always had to go his own way, you see. But I was keen on those thick volumes filled with pictures of heads. He loaned one to me, and I got handy at copying faces, if I do say so myself.

Rembrandt? Why, he made his very own paint box. Filled it with old brushes and bladders of paint that he filched when his Pa wasn't looking. I once asked to borrow some colors from Rembrandt, but learned my lesson quick enough. The sorry piece of a boy refused.

"Get to the kitchen where you belong," he said.

The next day, I found him sitting in Angelica's chair in the painting room. He was copying heads from her album, planning to pass the drawings off as his own. When I sashayed close by, he knew I'd seen his lying self. From then on, Rembrandt stayed out of my way. Sent me some monstrous cold looks, though.

The house was all a'flurry in those days. Angelica and Rembrandt in and out of the painting room, showing new drawings to Peale. Titian flying up and down the stairs from the carpentry room, taking cut fingers and bruises to Peggy Durgan. And two-year-old Rubens was fond of wearing paper masks while he chased Sophy around the dining room. One time Rafe came down to the kitchen to get off from the fray. Said he wanted to try a still life.

If you'll only give me a half a minute, Mag, I'll tell you what it is. Rafe rummaged through the pantry till he found a blue-striped bowl. Filled it with ripe peaches and set it on the table, then put a pitcher of cream to the side. A funnel of light from the window made the group of dishes purely glow, as if Rafe had created a special world of his own.

I was done hauling wood for the day and found a picture to copy from my book. The two of us settled at the table, Rafe with colored chalk and me with a pencil. We got to chewing over what we'd do when we got grown.

"Father predicts Rembrandt and I will be famous painters soon," Rafe said, bragging a bit. "He thinks all of Philadelphia will come to the museum for a Peale portrait."

Rafe turned a pear in the bowl so's a brown spot showed moist and spongy in the sun. I rubbed out the picture I'd drawn, as it was looking more like a squash than a head.

"Expect I'll be gone by then, Rafe. Don't forget, your pa promised to set me free if I work hard. B'lieve I'll go to oystering. Pick the ones big as my hand and make a lot of money. Maybe become the captain of a sailing ship." I was blustering some, too, but you know how nine-year-olds are, Maggie.

Rafe got quiet for a long minute. Laid his chalk down. "You're *too* hard a worker, Moze. Father told Mother he plans to keep you for a good many years."

It was as if I'd been catching a nod, and Rafe's words woke me up. Peale wasn't about to cut me loose. My friend could be a famous artist one day, but I couldn't see round the corner to the future. "Industry and perseverance" meant nothing at all, except that Peale would get the best of me, maybe for the next nineteen years.

A yeasty ball of resentment rose in my gullet—

putting the father's sins on the son, you see. Seemed like Rafe had everything—two parents to care for him, a handsome home, larning of all sorts. All I had were Peale's empty words.

I threw Rafe a black look, but held my tongue. If there's one thing I've learned, it's that you can feel two ways at once about someone. I was deep jealous of Rafe, yet beholden, too. That night in the kitchen, he had risked his daddy's anger to argue for my freedom, and though I wanted to forget it, I never could.

I guess that's why I hurt bad for him the next day. He proudly showed his still life to Peale in the painting room, and I tagged along. But there was a trap waiting for poor Rafe. When it came to still lifes, old Charley had a bunch in his britches.

Peale took one look and tossed the sketch aside. "No respectable artist makes still lifes," he said, "and no true lover of art would purchase one. They are mere monkey pictures. Any tolerable genius could paint them."

Rafe didn't seem to care a bit. He made an ape sound, scratched his armpits, and moseyed out. It plucked him, though, I could tell, for after that, he painted his foodstuffs on the sly.

I can't answer your question, girl. Rafe's early still life exercises must have disappeared. I haven't seen any round here for years, and it's a shame. Seemed like you could poke the paper and juice would dribble down. For all I know, Peale got rid of every one.

MARINE ROOM

DO NOT TOUCH THE BIRDS. THEY ARE COVERED WITH ARSENIC POISON. Heed the sign propped against the wall, Maggie! Don't be fingering any dead animals in here. You needn't ask again, girl, I mean it.

By summer of 1786, Peale's moving picture shows had lost their pull, and he was broke. So he finally opened his museum in July, hoping the "glorious repository" would bring in a good chunk of money.

Peale was true to his word about me helping out. Put me to work straight off, carting river sand and digging up sod. These he used to set up a mock grotto in the skylight room. It was his first museum display and an amusing sight, specially to me, a boy of ten.

The pond in the grotto was made of glass, with stuffed fish and waterfowl placed on banks behind it. Peale ringed the pond with a beach, where horny toads, water snakes, and turtles looked to be playing upon the sand. All of them dead as a dumbwaiter, of course. Trees, grass, and a ceiling of pretend rock finished off the natural-looking scene.

Peale charged visitors one shilling to view the display. He posted the warning sign to keep people's hands off the stuffed birds and fishes. Never did much good, as folks handled them, anyways.

Did *I* heed the warning? What kind of question is that to ask your old pa? Well, now, I did touch the red-legged pheasant, but only once. Just had to stroke his soft bright feathers, you know. Yanked my fingers away soon as they began to tingle.

You best light a candle before we go any farther, Mag. The lantern is low, and this is a peculiar room, full of shadows. A few of the staring beasts from Peale's grotto been stored up here for years. Stare right back if you're feeling skeery. Nothing except painted glass in those eyeholes.

The grotto was only the beginning of Peale's passion. He claimed if folks studied animals, they might understand their own selves better. Twould make them good citizens for their new country. And Peale, he aimed to teach them. SCHOOL OF WISDOM, says the bragging sign over the museum door.

As Peale's Lombard Street museum was the first public one in the United States, Americans were proud to help him out. Every day wild animals from North and South America were delivered to the backyard. Monkeys, a rhino, an anteater, a baboon, and other strange creatures I never saw before or since.

Peale tied the living critters in the empty lot next to the house. They had to be fully grown to be shot and stuffed, you see. Those animals kept me worn out. Twice a day I fed them—apples, asparagus, and mice, mostly—then raked up their turds in the morning.

Lost your craving for an apple, Mag? There's a curious feel to the air in here, I do agree.

The Peale boys cared for the caged varmints inside the house. Lizards and frogs and all. Had I been Peale, I'd a'never let Rembrandt near the animals. Not after the roguish boy threw a paint maul at his pet kitten and broke its tiny back. It didn't die, but it was a cruel sight, seeing that cat drag its hind legs round the house. You do have a way with words, Maggie. No, our Rembrandt was not a very appealing fellow.

Anyways, it was the dead beasts what people paid to see. They loved the stuffed cow. Don't gawk too long, or you'll sicken for sure. Poor freakish thing has five legs, three feet, and two tails. I milked that cow every day for years till finally it died. It was Rafe's idea of fun to show it suckling the stuffed two-headed calf.

The animals kept a'coming to Peale's Museum like it was old Norah's ark. Peale himself added birds and fish fast as he could cotch and stuff them. Took Rafe and me along on some hunting trips to help him out.

I specially recall one spring trek to the river marsh, as Charley was in a pertish mood on the ride there. He told stories about his days as an army captain and praised Rafe's sketches of the countryside.

When we got to the marsh, Peale stalked water witches in the shallows. Three times he sneaked down to the water, his skinny legs pumping like drumsticks. Then he stood stock-still, till he was close enough to shoot the pie-billed birds. That Charley, he was an odd duck, all right.

Meanwhile, Rafe and I worked in right good earnest. We landed us a two-foot string of kingfish and helped Peale preserve them. I'll tell you how he did it, Maggie, as I know you're commencing to ask.

First he stripped off every inch of skin with a sharp knife, going right over the top. Gouged the eyeballs out and pulled all flesh, fat, and bones away. Dragged the brains out through a hole in the fish's head. The flies loved the innards that piled up round our feet, but Rafe turned dead-white. Then Peale put us to work.

"Raphaelle, you mix the arsenical water," Peale said, "while I carve."

As vultures circled overhead, nagging us to let them eat alone, Rafe measured two pounds of arsenic into a large kettle and added three times as much water. Meanwhile, Peale cut a chunk of cork in the shape of the fish.

"Moses, you stir the mixture," he ordered. "When it settles, Raphaelle will dip each skin until it is fully soaked."

Rafe was still looking chalky, but he made the best of his task. As he swirled the skin in the water, he bulged his eyeballs and puckered his lips. Looked for all the world like a dying fish. I giggled, though the jest doesn't seem so funny now.

Peale covered the cork with the skin, added crystal eyes, and the job was done. Preserving was quick business—my, yes, Maggie, you could say those fish were Pealed.

This particular trip pleasured me greatly. It was a gift to get away from the stinking critters in Peale's yard, to let the April sun drench me down, but a darkness was rolling in that neither Rafe nor I could see. A few years later, when I took full measure of the day, it weighed heavy as strap iron upon my heart.

LECTURE ROOM

Hadn't been for Philis, I never would a'known what was coming down the pike. Let's go down to the lecture room, and we'll stop awhile on the risers. I'll tell you how I larnt to read Peale's tangled mind.

By December of 1786, Charley's museum was barely underway, and he was hard out of cash again. So broke, he borrowed money from Benjamin Rush to buy fifteen bushels of coal. Peale used the coal to better heat his freezing house, since some of the children upstairs had caught a chill. I was ailing, too. Had a vexatious cough what wouldn't go away.

Even with the loan, Peale still felt poor. One morning he appeared in the kitchen. "Philis, I want you to have your freedom," Peale said.

The words made my chest hurt even more. I swallowed hard. Was everyone in the world going free but me?

"I will give you a generous amount of time to raise fifty pounds."

Philis looked confused. "Fifty pounds, sir?"

"That is your price. The amount it will take to purchase yourself."

"But Mr. Peale," I broke in, coughing, "Philis has no way to find that kind of money!"

Charley's blue eyes narrowed. A ten-year-old slave doesn't tell the master what to do.

He ignored me and turned to Philis. "I have already refused one hundred pounds for you. Necessity compels me. I must have fifty to pay a debt at the board yard on Spruce Street."

So this was Peale's hollow offer of freedom! That's for certain, Mag. Dress a skunk up like a cat, he'll still smell like a skunk. Philis scrambled to get her money but never could, as she had no spare time to earn it. Nor did she have friends who could lend that large sum.

Seven months after Peale's offer, I got an even better look at the yellow underbelly of his hide. One hot day in July 1787, Charley sent Philis down to the Pennsylvania Society for Promoting the Abolition of Slavery and for the Relief of Free Negroes Unlawfully Held in Bondage and for Improving the Condition of the African Race. It was a stretched-out name, it's true, but it started with a simple idea: To make sure freed slaves were not kidnapped and sold back into bondage.

Peale wrote a letter for Philis to carry with her.

"Can you puzzle it out, Moses?" she asked before she left.

"A'course I can, Philis."

Grandly I took the letter and pronounced every

word pretty as you please. It related as how Philis was a mulatto woman with good character and few wants, and would the Society buy her for fifty pounds?

Now, the Quaker gentlemen of the Society warn't likely to pay Peale for Philis. Their job was to free slaves, not buy them. He must a'been in grievous need to try such a thing. Maybe he couldn't face them straight out, since his friend, Benjamin Franklin, was president of the Society, so he sent Philis, instead.

She came back that afternoon looking glum. Shook the dust from her skirts and dipped a drink of cool springwater from the bucket.

"Those folks were cross and ill-natured, Moses. They said Peale was rich enough to free me himself."

You're exactly right, Mag. The Society had no business abusing Philis, and Peale had no gumption to him at all, forcing a slave to act as her own slave trader!

That night, Philis carried on till I hardly knew what to do.

"I've no hope of buying myself," she wept. "The worst part is not knowing Peale's new plan. Since this one didn't work, is he fixing to sell me to some spiteful master?"

I was not yet eleven and she was twenty-six, but her tears made me feel like she was the child, and I was the grown-up man.

"It's hard to tell what Peale thinks about slavery,

Philis. Sometimes he seems against it, other times
. . . well, he let Ma and Pa go, and I believe he'll do
the same for you."

Of course, he kept me, I said to myself, but I
wanted to give Philis hope, so I held the thought
inside. Yes, that's a fitting way to put it, Maggie.
When it came to slavery, Peale was neither fish nor
fowl.

The following day I stumbled on a way I might
help Philis. Can't say that I was proud of it, as I
knew Ma would switch me for sure if she found
out. Round mid-morning, Peale and his youngest
children were in the painting room.

"Moses," he called down, "we need a pot of tea!"

Philis fixed the tray, and as I carried it past
Peale's bedroom chamber, I saw two books sitting
on his desk. Being newly charmed by the wonders
of reading, I slipped in to peek at the words.

One was bound in leather, the pages filled with
copies of letters Peale had written over the years.
T'other was an old diary ending in 1780, the year
we moved to Lombard. I almost slammed the
books shut, thinking that reading his private papers
was like stealing.

Then I thought again. Hadn't he stolen me
from my ma and pa? Wasn't he stealing Philis from
herself? When I remembered Philis, that put the
ball in the cannon. Maybe Peale's papers would tell
me his plans for her. Knowing Rachel might waltz
in at any time, I flipped the pages faster'n Philis
could flip roasted taters on the hearth.

No, Mag, I didn't discover anything new. Just that Peale was a miserable speller. And a letter he wrote to the committee after they turned her away. Explaining how he'd given her a "considerable time to raise the sum of £50 to purchais her freedom."

Once I started reading, though, I couldn't help myself. The word "slaves" in a diary entry caught my eye. In 1778, Peale criticized some Army officers from Virginia. He said owning slaves had made them "laisy." Yet in a letter that same year he wrote, "I have a desire to purchase the Negro Boy who speaks French to wait on me, I have long wanted one." No, Maggie, Charley wasn't worried about turning lazy himself.

When I heard Rachel's silk slippers on the stairs, I eased the door shut and took the tray to the painting room. Peale was showing Rembrandt how to grind red vermilion powder and helping Angelica draw a beaked nose.

After Charley thanked me proper, I went back to the kitchen with two pictures in my head. One of him leaned over his young ones, patient and proud. The other was of Philis, weeping pitiful the night before.

Puts you in mind of the effigy, Mag? I can see why. Like Benedict Arnold, Peale had two faces. One he showed to the world—family man, soldier, painter, scientist, museum master. And one lying face only his diary and slaves could see.

Shortly after that, Peale asked Peggy Durgan to do the housekeeping. Then he up and sold Philis, turning her over to a farmer north of town. The night before she left, I made her sit by the fire so's I could draw her face. Sketched it twice, giving her one as a good-bye gift and saving t'other for myself.

Don't know. I stashed it some place safe, but forget where. I'm glad I kept something of Philis though, as I never saw her again.

QUADRUPED ROOM

I wish I'd never snooped around Peale's diaries, Mag. Because I wish to God I'd not larnt about the poison. But reading his papers got to be like chewing tobaccy. Made me sickish at first, then I couldn't chase it from my mind.

Sometimes I even copied the pages, underlined the interesting parts, and hid them away. Helped me feel like I owned a piece of him, you see. Yet the more I read, the less I understood the man.

On June twenty-seventh, 1788, Peale wrote, "I employ my self in preserving one hen Red-Bird and a Cock & Hen of a specis of Wood red-Bird." That same evening he was afflicted with "very severe head ack."

He had a similar problem on July ninth. "Began & continued my Labour this whole day in washing my Birds & Beasts in the Arsenic Water, having my hands continually wet, I find a considerable soreness at the ends of my fingers, so much that I had a small fever at night & some restlessness."

After preserving a wood drake in September,

Charley was stricken again. "Last night I was attacked with a violent Colick, I puked, and was Worked downwards," he wrote. "I am not well at the time of writing this—not clear of a fever the whole day."

It seemed peculiar that Charley would handle arsenic when it plainly was what made him ill, but I guess he was so taken with the museum that nothing could stop him. He even dipped big carcasses in the brew with a long-handled broom, then stuffed them with hempen material.

You can see what I mean here in the Quadruped Room. Hundreds of four-footed creatures are coming on thick. Stopped dead in their tracks, as if playing a game of everlasting tag. Wander round, if you like, but try not to drift too far.

I see you eyeing the Missouri grizzlies. See the big one on the left? He escaped from his cage one summer night. Took a shine to one of Peale's monkeys and ripped his arms clean off. Charley shot and stuffed the wild brute straight away. Mounted him alongside his mate.

Why, yes, Maggie, twas me in charge of the bear's cage. I don't rightly recall how the animal got loose. You ask stout questions for such a slender girl!

While Charley was out hunting wood drakes, his wife had another daughter. The birthing left Rachel with a pain in her side and a tightening-up cough. She felt so puny, she seldom got out of bed.

Her sickness put a long face on the family, but I had my own worriments after Ma visited Lombard one cool fall day.

I had just mucked out the stalls and was grooming the horses, jobs Peale gave me when Pa went free. Poplar leaves were falling like yellow hearts, their sour smell mixed with the stench of the soiled straw.

The gate latch clicked open and Ma rounded the corner of the stable. Though her footsteps were firm, she had a forsaken air about her. Looked shabby, too, her bodice held together with old knotted cord. A threadbare edge of shift showed underneath, gray from too many washings.

"Rest yourself, Ma," I said, pulling up a bale of hay.

"Can't stay long, Moses. I've a mess of shirts to scrub and iron." She shivered when the wind gusted. "You should know your daddy has signed up as a sailor on a packet. The coaster runs twixt Charleston and Boston, picking up passengers and cargo along the way."

I stuck the currycomb in the horse's mane. "Ma, why?!"

"On account of the money, son."

"But you'll be alone for weeks at a time!"

"I'll have plenty of company. A newly freed family has moved in to share my rooms."

Ma was matter-of-fact about it, but I knew she and Pa were closer than a hot biscuit to melted butter. Many a night I'd heard her crawl in next to him, her voice softening as she warmed her cold toes on his shins.

"As long as they're sharing the rent, too . . ."

"That, and the cost of food."

And before I could warn her not to work so hard, she was gone, her short legs cutting a swath through the crispy leaves.

As if Pa's leaving wasn't enough to occupy my thoughts, Rembrandt quit school when he turned thirteen. He like to drove me crazy. Strutted about the house all day, bragging on a portrait he was painting of himself. It was a fair to middling picture, I'll admit. A good likeness that showed his shifty rooster eyes.

Seemed like Rembrandt always ended up in the painting room, which left Raphaelle to help Peale on hunting trips and stuff animals when they got home. I knew Rafe d'ruther paint still lifes than skin dead fish and birds, but we know how Peale felt about still lifes, and by now, Rafe was always under his daddy's thumb.

It was while Rafe and Peale were hunting snakes in Delaware that my world turned dismal dark. One frosty evening early in 1790, a colored girl brought a message to the kitchen door. She was fresh out of breath. "Your ma says come straight to Elbow Lane!"

Something was terrible wrong. Often I'd slip away to the alley for a Sunday visit, usually in the evening, so Ma couldn't drag me with her to morning church service. But not once in four years had she sent for me.

I asked Peggy Durgan could I leave, since Peale was gone and Rachel was a'bed, wasting away. Peggy said yes, of course, and I bolted the ten blocks up to Elbow Lane.

Snow was falling like flour from a sifter. Drifting so heavy, I almost slipped into the Dock Creek canal. Ma was grieving hard when I arrived, too numb to cry, but ready to fall out all the same.

"I just got word, son. Your Pa's boat sunk two weeks ago. It was caught leeward in a storm and splintered upon the shoals off Cape Fear, North Carolina. All hands aboard gone down with it."

The news struck me senseless. Pa wasn't one for talk, but there's more ways than one to speak of love. I always knew he was proud of me, and he'd have walked to hell and back for Ma. My daddy was dependable as the tide. I never thought that one time he'd die.

Don't stew, Mag—I'll be around till you've got a husband and babies of your own, I promise you that.

There was nothing to do about a burying, not with Pa's body on the bottom of the unforgiving sea. The next day, Richard Allen gave a talk at Saint George's and preached some soothing words. Still, Ma was awful cut up that Pa had no proper funeral.

"Your daddy's spirit will never rest," she moaned on the way back to Elbow Lane. "He'll wander forever, looking to join his elders."

Fact is, Ma went right crazed for a few days. Told me she heard Pa sighing when it was nothing but the wailing wind. Said he was crying "Lucy!" when it was only a lonesome hooty owl.

Me, I felt closer to the troubles of the living, such as what Ma would do for money. I knew she'd get widow's aid from the Free African Society, the one Preacher Allen had started the year before. But Pa was never coming home, and she needed a steady income for the years ahead.

A scheme took shape in my mind, and like everything else in my boyhood, it circled around Charles Willson Peale. Charley had extra cash after selling Philis, and the museum was bringing in some, too. He had made a pledge when he set my folks free. Said he'd loan them money if they needed it. Now it was time to recollect those words to him.

When I returned to Lombard Street two days later, I ran into Rafe in the front hall, just back from Delaware. "Peggy told me about your father, Moze," he said. "I regret that he died." Rafe was never comfortable with solemn talk, but I knew he meant the words.

I was too hell-bent on my errand to stop for long. "Where's your pa, Rafe? I need to speak to him straight off."

"Upstairs, in the carpentry room," said Rafe.

Sure enough, there was Peale, kneeling over a four-foot rattler stretched full-out on the floor.

"Mr. Peale," I tippy-toed around the subject, "you know, my ma's a fair good cook."

"From the throat to the anus, one hundred and sixty-four." Peale's spectacles slid down his nose while he counted the belly scales. He surely didn't like folks breaking into his study time.

"Now that Pa's gone, I been thinking she should start her own business. Rent out a stall in the covered market and sell pepper-pot soup."

"Twenty-three from the anus to the tail." He pushed up the spectacles.

"So I was wondering—could you see your way clear to help her out? Loan her rent money every month till she gets set up proper?"

"One rattle and another forming . . ."

I hung on, Maggie, as if Peale were a bullhead wiggling on a pole.

"Like you promised four years ago when you freed Ma and Pa!"

This last I said with some muscle in my voice, though I felt wobbly as an egg in water. Peale finally looked up from the snake. I could see tired lines of worry sprangling down his face. The nearness of death can tassle the living together in surprising ways. With a dying wife, Charley must have felt weighted down his own self. He knew I missed Pa, same as he would miss Rachel if she went.

He straightened up and spoke real kind. "Tell Lucy to inquire about the amount of rent. I'll send it to her each month as long as I can."

Then he gave me a rare smile.

"Your mother will earn money in good time, Moses. Her soup is the best in the city, and certainly better than the chicken soup I have prepared since Philis left."

I wasn't of a mind to dwell on Philis, not with Peale, anyway. I thanked him and rushed up to Elbow Lane with the news. Ma and I would always be lonesome for Pa, but at least she wouldn't end up in the almshouse. You know the place, girl. That sprawling three-story building near Spruce. The one where free blacks and poor Irish go when they're sick, hungry, or need a place to die.

Part II:
Long room –
Portrait side

A round this corner is the Long Room, Maggie. Here's a picture of it that Peale drew a few years back. Between these whitewashed walls is the center of the museum and the heart of my tale. Let's stroll down the right side, past the birds. We'll walk up the window side after we tour the Mammoth Room.

Here now. See the rows of bird cases? Trotting across the top are portraits. A number of dry-faced generals, but you'll find some of Peale's people peering down at us, too. There's a picture of Charley's first wife, finished a little bit before she died.

RACHEL

Rachel, she got very low in February of 1790, short to the time Pa drowned. The day before she left this world, she asked her oldest children to come nigh. Hugged Rembrandt and Raphaelle as best she could with her reedy arms.

"Be dutiful to your father," she whispered. "Mind him always and follow his advice." Rafe took her words too much to heart, I'm sorry to say.

Now, Mag, I didn't mean to make you cry. Forgive me, girl, I know you're remembering your mama's long tussle with consumption. Yes, I'll finish this part quick-like.

It was lung problems what took Rachel off, too. When she died on April 12, 1790, there was a snuffling quiet in the house. Rembrandt went silent to bed. Never said a word about his mama's leaving. Rafe came to the kitchen to console himself with a still life.

"What have you got for me to paint, Moze?" he asked. Red cracks lined his eyeballs, and his voice was weary.

I handed him some leeks from the larder. "Sorry about your ma, Rafe, but at least you got to say good-bye to her." Pa's passing was a raw hurt, and I couldn't help thinking that things always worked out better for Rafe, even death.

He piled three apples in a bowl and set the leeks against the rim, real careful-like.

"Father won't allow anyone in the room, not even Peggy Durgan. I begged to see Mother's face one more time, but he never listens to me."

Twas true enough, Maggie. Peale watched his dead wife for three days, refusing to believe she was gone. Wouldn't let anybody touch her thin body. Kept looking for her to twitch a finger or open an eye. Wasn't that just like Peale? He never could see the truth for looking straight at it.

BETSY

Peale was cut up powerful by Rachel's death. With six children, though, he couldn't let feelings get in the way of practical business. By summer of 1790, he was out of blast again. He hit out for Maryland, taking Rafe with him on a five-month trip.

As usual, Peale aimed to make money painting portraits and scare up new animals for the museum. This time he was hunting something extra: Another wife. Peale needed a mama for his young ones, since they were running wild without Rachel. Considering his large number of children, I suspect he couldn't go too long without coupling, neither.

I remember well the day before his leaving, because he insisted I clean the museum room top to bottom. Charley had me scrub the yellow-pine floors, wash windows, and all as that. Late in the afternoon, when I was more than ready to quit, he decided to clean the grotto, too.

"Moses, mop the glass pond," he commanded. "I'll dust the stuffed birds with a feather."

We worked silently until I noticed his face was covered with sweat.

"You're looking awful peaked, Mr. Peale," I said. Peale groaned, like something had grabbed his innards.

"Finish up, will you?" he asked.

He left the room doubled-over, mumbling something about working his bowels with castor oil. Though Charley was still waxy the next morning, his remedy must have worked, since he had me up at dawn to pack his travel chest.

"Put in six plain shirts, three pairs of striped stockings, and four cravats for Raphaelle," ordered Peale. "For me, pack four new ruffled shirts, four old ones, nine extra socks, two neck handkerchiefs, two pairs of spotted cotton stockings, and three pairs of silk."

I think you're right, Mag. Our Charley was a mite vain and wanted to be presentable for the ladies. He went through four in Maryland before finding one to his liking, a twenty-five-year-old, name of Betsy. That's her picture up there, hanging over the stuffed eagle. Plump as a two-crust pie she was. Betsy was plain all right, but she had a firm voice. The family called her "Mother General," and whatever she said was the thing done.

After Peale married her in May 1791, life on Lombard Street smoothed out level as the river on a summer day. The younger children settled down, and Peale retired from the portrait business. That's when he started pushing his sons to paint pictures of quality folks and government men.

Though Rembrandt took right to it, Rafe never liked it much. Those fancy-pants people were mighty serious about themselves, and who could blame them, since portraits cost dearly. But Rafe, he'd joke and play till they got most insulted. It was his downfall that he preferred to paint cabbage heads than heads of state any day.

LUCY

Now then. This part of the story has left me wind-less. Slide your hunkers over and let me take a rest on the stool. I want to show you a special portrait.

Time came when Peale almost killed me, and Ma might have died, too. No, it was nothing like that, Mag. No weapons, just an idea white folks have. Think they can use up black people and throw them away.

This picture of your granny at the market will help tell the tale. Twas sketched by some fellow from the newspaper.

I've kept a copy in my wallet all these years. It's stained a bit from the leather, and the ink's rubbed clean off. But if you look close, you can see that everyone—black and white, young and old—prized Lucy Williams's spicy chowder. "Pepper pot, smoking hot!" she cried every day, perched on a stool with a ladle in hand.

It all started in the summer of 1793. Come late August, my seventeenth birthday as I recall, I decided to visit Ma at her stall.

PEPPER POT.

" Pepper Pot, smoking hot."

Strangers who visit the city, cannot but be amused with the cries of the numerous black women who sit in the market house and at the corners, selling a soup which they call pepperpot. It is made chiefly of tripe, ox-feet, and other cheap animal substances, with a great portion of spice. It is sold very cheap, so that a hungry man may get a hearty meal for a few cents. The print affords a good view of the group that often assemble around the tub, truly smoking hot, and excepting to weak stomachs, it is a very pleasant feast.

I have the clearest recollection of that walk. There'd been heavy rains, a good crop of mosquitoes, then a dusty drought. As I drew near the market, the smell of rotting sheep's heads and cattle guts almost made me lose my oatmeal. The place was near empty, and no wonder!

When I couldn't find Ma, I headed to Elbow Lane, and what I saw there was hard to believe. Your granny met me at the doorway, but wouldn't let me in. She looked like she'd been through the hackles. The free coloreds who shared her rooms were in lively suffering, she said. Yellow fever, it was, the most ungodly plague ever visited upon this city.

Her red bandanna was faded with sweat. "Folks been bad here for days, Moses," she told me. "First sign is yellowish eyeballs and a grainy black vomit. After the puking comes a slow, moanful sighing. Then they go off their heads, babbling like babies larning to talk."

Ma softened her voice so the dying inside couldn't hear. "Their faces turn purplish and look ready to burst with blood. Before long, they're gone. Sometimes death comes the second day. Sometimes eight days pass before Jesus calls them."

"Where are the bodies taken?" I asked, not really wanting to know, but too muddled to say more.

"Death cart comes by every night. Carries them to a pauper's trench in Potter's Field."

The news gave me a prickly feeling, like my shirt had dried with soap still in it. I loosened my neck scarf and looked up Elbow Lane. The fifteen-foot-wide alley was too quiet by far. No little shavers playing leapfrog, or handbarrow wheels slicking through the mud.

"Ma, you can't stay here! Come back to Lombard Street with me," I begged. "Nobody's sick down there!"

"Peale might not like it. Might think I was spreading disease."

"Peale's not even home, Ma. He sent Rafe on a preserving trip to Georgy, then took Betsy and the youngest children to Delaware. He left Angelica in charge of the others—I'm sure she won't mind."

"I won't do it, boy," she replied. "I won't risk giving the fever to them. Besides, there's a husband here who can't nurse his wife, and a mother too sick to care for her baby. After all, the Bible says this is the Christian thing to do."

Ma ordered me back to Lombard straight off. Told me to close the windows and stay in the house. I'll go clean to my grave remembering the fearful look that rimmed her eyes. How she told me to get along, then shut the door on me, quick as you please. It was against my wishes Mag, but I yielded, as there was nothing else to do when your granny got a salty tone in her voice.

By early September, the pestilence had spread over the city. Every time I went to the window, I saw a steady stream of folks leaving by wagon and on foot. Soon there was no one to cart the bodies away. One time I opened the door and looked up and down Lombard. Corpses littered the street like stray pieces of trash.

Heard later that even President George Washington fled, along with his Secretary of State, Thomas Jefferson. I'd a'left, too, and taken Ma with me, had I only been free to go.

Only one newspaper stayed in print during those ticklish times. That's where I read some whites believed black people were immune to the plague. Said their African blood protected them. If they'd been to Elbow Lane they'd have known different, would have known that it was your granny's goodness and faith that kept her there tending to the sick. But white people don't cut through that alley too regular.

BENJAMIN RUSH

Here's the portrait of Peale's friend, Benjamin Rush. Yes, he was a fine-figured man, but not a smart doctor, as it turns out. When I heard that Rush was asking for black volunteer nurses to bleed and purge white patients during the fever, I worked up a slather of worry. Bad enough that Ma was nursing her friends. I hoped she had the good sense not to try to heal all of Philadelphia.

There was no way to find out unless I went up to Elbow Lane, and to tell the truth, I couldn't risk it. No, it wasn't fear of the fever that troubled me. Twas what Ma might do if I disobeyed her orders to stay put.

In the midst of the panic, Peale brought Betsy and the children home. Following an advisement in the newspaper, old Charley sprinkled vinegar on the furniture and set off musket charges to keep the fever away. Two members of the household caught it anyhow.

It hit Betsy first. Peale gave her a gentle cure of boiled barley water and flaxseed enemas, though he almost lost her when the purple blotches came and she began to drool blood. Shortly after, my guts started to heave. Before long, I was raving on my pallet in the kitchen.

I disremember most of this time, excepting my head felt thick as Peale's fish glue. Once I thought the poplar trees outside were dancers twisting in the breeze. Silver-bottomed leaves flipping this way and that, like ladies' skirts in a reel.

Benjamin Rush had devised a strong cure for the fever—calomel enemas that produced large evacuations, dark in color. No one was sure if the cure really worked, so Peale decided to experiment on me. It was almost as if I were one of his mute animals.

Now, he never let me lay in the muck, I will admit. Carried the mess pot away every day and let fresh air in the kitchen each evening. He nursed Betsy with the milder cure and me with Rush's till he hardly changed clothes for two weeks. Even got a touch of the fever himself. Was he nursing me out of kindness or need? It's a good question, Mag.

Whatever his purpose, it was a gosh awful harsh remedy. To this day, there's doctors in Philadelphia who say Rush murdered patients with his "heroic" cure, and it damn nigh killed your daddy. The fever did leave me in late September, so I guess I must be thankful for that. But whether it was Rush's cure healed me, I'll never know.

By then, I was mighty enfeebled and thinking for sure that Ma must be with Pa. Specially after I heard that heaps of coloreds were dropping all over the city, sick as any white folks. And this next thing will tear you up, Mag. One day on the street I heard some whites accusing the volunteer black nurses of thievery. Isn't that something?

I hauled myself up Elbow Lane soon as I was able. Makes me tired to remember that moonless night. The streets were empty except for the bodies of rotting cats. Houses vacant, shops boarded up. For nine blocks, I hardly saw a living soul and was already sorrowing when I reached Ma's shack. Expecting to hear her body had been tossed in a common grave.

There's no need to tell you I went wild with relief when I opened the door. Your granny was huddled in a rocker, ragged but free of fever. She didn't feel much like talking. Just sipped cider while I told her about my own struggles with the fever.

Then she roused herself enough to speak. Like I feared, she had stepped forward when the call went out for help.

"Son, you wouldn't believe all the truth if I was to tell you. The things I witnessed in the streets. These cautious times bring out the worst in people. I saw a white woman who wouldn't lay a corpse in a coffin without six pounds' pay first. And a white nurse skulked out of a house, wearing a dead patient's rings."

I didn't have the heart to tell Ma the news. That folks were making out good people like her wanted to wrangle money from the sick and dying, too!

Tuck that lower lip in, girl. No use talking up a ruction to me. Instead, you pass the word on if anybody asks—during the yellow fever epidemic of 1793, it was only prayer and Philadelphia's black volunteers what held the city together.

By November of 1793, the city was breathing regular again. Thousands of folks straggled back to their houses and jobs. Peale even took up portrait-painting again, as he'd lost money when the museum closed due to lack of visitors.

Ma went back to work, too, but like other poor folk, she was in sore need of cash after the epidemic. Earned enough for eats and clothes but still needed rent money for the stall. She was hoping to rustle on her own, though we both knew that day was locked up in the future. Might not come till I was freed and could help her out.

Now swing the lantern toward the end wall, Maggie, and you'll spy a door that goes nowhere . . . what's the matter? You look like you've seen a devil baby! Those are no ghosts—that's a painting of Raphaelle and Titian climbing some pretend steps.

Staircase Group

Calm down, and we'll take a closer look. Wait up, now. You're liable to crack a knuckle if you try to pick up the museum ticket on the stair tread—it's nothing but dabs of paint.

When Peale made this picture, he got carried away. Hung a door frame around it so it looked real. And, yes, that's a genuine step at the bottom. Go on, then, climb it. See if you don't raise a knot on your head when you hit the wall behind the canvas.

Charley thought his trick-of-the-eye art could fool people. He even bragged that George Washington tipped his hat when he passed by the painting. But Peale's art didn't fool me—in fact, it showed his real self as clearly as his diaries did.

Well, now. If you'll recall, Rafe was gone during the fever. Off hunting animals in Georgy. He returned in late 1793, shortly after the sickness had passed. We caught up on news as I unpacked his travel chest.

"What did you find in Georgy, Rafe?" His clothes were a tangled mess. Torn and stained as a twelve-year-old boy's.

"I caught and preserved quite a few birds," said Rafe. He flopped on the bed, pulled his boots off, and wiggled his toes. "And how is your health, Moze? Betsy said Father nursed you both during the epidemic."

The boots were coated with mud and horse dung. I put them outside the door so's I could clean them later in the kitchen.

"That he did, Rafe, that he did." I didn't go into details. What good would it do to tell him that, cured or not, his daddy had treated me as less than human? A son doesn't want to believe such about his father.

Rafe stretched out on the bed. "It's good to find everyone alive after the fever. I only wish I could stay longer."

"You're leaving again? And here at Christmastime!"

"Father has planned an extensive trip to South America for me. In a few days I shall travel to French Guiana in South America, then on to Mexico. He says the museum needs specimens from that part of the world."

I tied Rafe's laundry in a sheet and set it on the floor. There was something plucking at me, but I couldn't peg it down. A trip or two to help stuff fish and birds was one thing. But now Rafe was toting the weight of preserving, and for months at a time.

Charley knew arsenic fumes and dust were bad. He'd worried about it for himself in the diaries. How could a father keep setting his own flesh and blood on the road to sickness?

"Why is it always you to make the longest trips and stuff the most animals?" I asked.

"I have not been singled out, Moses! Father has demonstrated the skill to the others—Rembrandt on occasion, Titian, and even Sophy and little Rubens. He says teaching his children the art of preserving is his favorite undertaking."

Still, I knew Rafe got nailed with the bulk of the risky work, and that Rembrandt seldom had to dip his precious hands in a pot of poison.

"Rafe, let me ask you something. Do you remember the time back in August of '90? When you and your daddy went off to Maryland for five months?"

My friend chuckled. He unbuttoned his shirt and flung it on the floor. My, yes, Maggie, slavery and Peggy Durgan had spoiled Rafe something awful. I wanted to kick his lazy self across the room. Instead, I untied the bundle and shoved the shirt in, wondering why I still bothered to worry about a slaveholder's son.

"How could I forget those months? The way Father circled around the widows like a young buck. My own *pater,* a balding man of forty-nine!"

"Do you recall how sick he was when the two of you left?"

"Indeed I do! We stopped along the road several times so he could empty his bowels in the bushes. On one occasion, he asked me to gather blackberries in my hat. He was convinced the ripe fruit would cure him of colic."

"Rafe, the day before the trip, your pa and I were in the grotto together. It was arsenic dust on the birds that made him sick. I witnessed it myself. You should take care with that poison."

Rafe, he was as good as his daddy at hiding from the truth. He just laughed and asked if there was something tasty in the kitchen to eat. Yes, I know, the arsenic was powerful bad stuff, yet how could I say more, Maggie, if Rafe didn't want to listen? How could I admit I'd read Peale's papers on the sly?

"But you hate preserving," I persisted. "Maybe you could talk Rembrandt into taking your place on this South America trip."

Rafe turned serious then. "I made a promise to Mother. A solemn deathbed vow to mind Father and follow his advice. If he advises me to go to South America, I shall go."

And you'd hack off a finger, I thought, if he gave you a smile in return.

The night before Rafe left, I was lying on my pallet. It was the go-to-sleep hour when thoughts streak through your mind like falling stars. When truth can bust you in the head, but you don't feel it yet.

Why Rafe, why Rafe? How come Peale pushes him toward the poison at home or away? And Rembrandt stays in the painting room to set his palette?

Then it swings at me, big and plain as a side of pork. It's fine enough for Peale to make fool-the-eye art, like the Staircase Group, but not Rafe. No difference, really, between still lifes that no one would buy and some of Peale's own mishaps—the Triumphal Arch disaster, the etchings that didn't sell, the moving pictures show that went broke.

It's painting respectable portraits Peale returns to, time and again. Portaits that prove he is more than a common craftsman and save his hide from scandal and debt. So it's portraits his sons should paint, too.

Suddenly the memory of Peale's calomel cure was strong in my mouth. Is Charley testing the effects of arsenic on his son, I wondered, like he tested Rush's remedy on me? You're a quick one, girl. If Rembrandt should die in the experiment, it would leave him to bring glory to the family name. Rembrandt, with his stiff portraits and smug ambition.

I tossed on my blanket, trying to think it through. When sleep didn't come, I slipped outside to check the animals. Some were scratching at their chains, wide awake and restless just like me.

I'd already tried talking to Rafe. Should I face Peale with it? Put it to him plain I knew how bad the arsenic was?

The wind was blowing rash and cleared my head of that idea. A slave doesn't go messing around in slaveholder business without paying a price. If Peale and I argued, he might sell me off like Philis. I could be held forever by another master, when I was already worse than a pig after molasses for my freedom.

It was your granny's situation that finally decided me. I had to mind my words. Couldn't chance Peale cutting off her rent money, not when she was just getting back on her feet after the fever crisis.

Quit breaking in, girl! Yes, yes, I was steaming some, too. Tired of picking up after Rafe, tired of cleaning his fine leather boots. I wanted to be free! To have a good strong notion of how it felt to own my body. I was disgusted with Peale and jealous of Rafe. The feelings blew together in my mind like wind and rain, till I couldn't separate the two.

So I held off. Rafe was my friend, but he was a Peale. If he were to figure out anything, he'd have to figure it out for himself, things being what they were for Ma and me. I couldn't tie our lives to Charley's shame and pride.

Jealousy, shame, and pride. These are the devil's horses, girl. They ride the world, and I guess they always will. Yes, that just about tells it.

RUBENS

Rafe returned from the jungles of South America in April of 1794. After all my worrying, I was surprised when he looked well enough. Brought back a stuffed toucan, a stuffed wildcat, and was as funny as ever, though what young man wouldn't be full of himself at the age of twenty? His spirits were so high, he took Rubens under his wing.

The ten-year-old was still the runt of Peale's litter. Every day he perched on my shoulder like a pet monkey while I carried him to school. Rafe babied him, too. Made the young fellow mascot of his militia unit, and painted this portrait of him, all dollied up in a blue uniform.

After seeing Rafe so perky, I thought maybe toiling for Charley had made me a little cuckoo. Every time I considered the poison, it seemed too ugly to be true, so I put the notion away for a while, and fixed my mind on hating slavery.

By the spring of 1794, Peale's displays were overflowing the Lombard Street house. He did some fast talking with the government folks.

Convinced them to let him move the displays to Philosophical Hall—the second home of Peale's Museum.

Fine, the government told him. Said he and his family could live there, too, if a kitchen was built in the basement, and I don't have to tell you who slept down there.

By June, Peale was ready to make the move and charged me with leading the way. As always he had what he took to be a clever idea. He yoked a stuffed bison to my shoulders, just like I was a poled ox. A passel of neighborhood boys followed behind, each one carrying another of the stuffed animals.

We made quite a sight, trotting down the street in a drove. People on Lombard flew to the doors and windows to watch as our cavalcade marched ten blocks up to the Walnut Street gate, then snaked into Philosophical Hall. Peale was tickled with the free publicity for the museum. Happy he'd lost only one alligator in the move.

It was humiliating, parading with little boys and pop-eyed creatures, I can tell you that, Mag. But Peale didn't concern himself with my humiliation. Proof to me that he still saw me as a boy, not the man I had become.

Charley kept his live animals chained inside the walled yard. He got himself two new bears and built a house just for them, with two parrots and a sign perched on top: FEED ME DAILY AND I'LL LIVE ONE HUNDRED YEARS, read the sign. It was meant as a joke to the customers, but it was me who fed them, always me!

Sorry, girl, I don't mean to yell. Brings me to a white heat yet, thinking about the years after we left Lombard. I was a young man of eighteen, but still feeding critters and raking up dung like I did when I was ten. Feeling caught as one of Peale's mounted fish. Eyes open, but still no future to look at.

Got so's I'd loiter about the tippling house across the street, looking for a comely girl. Don't ever let me catch you over there, Maggie, as you can't trust a fellow who's been in a grog shop.

Anyways, I'd swig a gill of rum, then go back to my hateful feeding chores. One evening I made a mean game of it. Instead of apples, I tossed wads of spitty tobaccy into the baboon's gaping mouth. The surprised look in his round eyes gave me a cruel pleasure.

Would Peale ever let me go? I wondered as I softened another plug in my cheek. I'll release you when you can maintain yourself, he liked to say, but it was Peale's Museum that needed maintenance, not Moses Williams. No, I had to do Charley's bidding, and so did Rafe.

GEORGE
WASHINGTON

Which circles me back to the claw of the thing, as Ma used to say. See the picture of President Washington? The one in the frame that's as thick as your hand? I'd bet a dove a'setting that you can't guess who painted it. Oh, Mag, you got a laugh sweetern' honey cake when you think you know something, but you don't know how the painting came about, so hush up while I tell it.

Washington agreed to let the Peales take his portrait in 1795. Tradition said the choice assignment should have gone to the oldest boy, and twould have been a prize job. Folks would surely give their portrait business to Rafe if it was known he painted the country's greatest hero.

But, no, Charley handed the plum assignment to Rembrandt. Let his mulish second son have the best seat, directly in front of the president. Peale sat next to Rembrandt to give him encouragement and advice.

Rafe? He didn't even come in till the second sitting. Hung off to the back and sketched a watercolor of Washington's face. My friend got skunked out of his big chance to shine, and that was the end of that.

Rembrandt's portrait showed Washington as an old codger with sagging jaws and droopy skin. Still, it became all the thing, and Rembrandt made ten copies to sell. His original has been hanging here all these years. No, I never saw Rafe's watercolor again. It got lost somewhere in these museum rooms, just like Rafe.

Tore me pretty near to pieces when Rafe made no insistence about Washington's painting. Seeing him cave in like that to old Charley and Rembrandt coming out on top. I took it in my head to talk some sense into him about Peale's domineering ways.

The morning after Washington's last sitting, I asked Rafe to meet me in front of the Black Bear Inn. Warn't many folks about, as it was too early for strong waters. A few washerwomen on their rounds. A couple of black men in top hats and tails setting up clam carts by the curb.

Soon as Rafe reached the corner, I grabbed him and blessed him out.

"You got to larn to stand flat-footed against your pa!" I preached. "Should a'been you painting Washington's picture, not Rembrandt!"

"What's bitten you, Moze? Rembrandt attends art classes every day, and he uses the painting room more than anyone else in the family. Perhaps Father chose Rembrandt because he is the finer painter."

"Didn't you want to paint the president in oil?" I asked, digging a little deeper. Hoping the taunt would make him mad enough to change. "Didn't you think you could do it?"

A little shadow of hurt ran through Rafe's eyes, but as usual, he waltzed around his feelings. "I don't care all that much about portraits, Moze. Rembrandt likes the folderol. Let him have what he desires."

It went all over me that Rafe didn't have enough gumption to see what I saw. Talent shining like a gold button on a cloak of blue. Rembrandt, he was a no-count artist compared to Rafe. Rafe's pictures always fooled the eye. The colors were prettier, too.

He smiled and gave me a friendly clout on the back. "To tell the truth, Moze, I long sometimes to forget about portraits. To be a boy again, skating and fishing with you."

Then before I could say more, he aimed me toward the grog shop. "My friend," he declared, "let's have a game of billiards!"

And just like in the old days, we loafed for hours. Though Peale didn't approve of mimicry at all, Rafe had taken a fancy to it. He made the billiard balls talk during our game, and I wish you could'a heard it, girl.

"I am sore hit!" one ball cried pitiful from the end of the green felt table.

From the corner pocket another squeaked, "Save me! I'm buried alive!"

Caused a ruckus with the other customers, I'll

say that. They bought rounds for Rafe and me, and by late afternoon we were in our cups. Neither of us had a worry when we walked back to Philosophical Hall.

Now, Maggie, you wipe that look off your face. Puts me in mind of your ma before I gave up the drink for good. Mouth shriveled up like you've been sucking a sour ball. Last thing I need tonight is a lecture from my own daughter.

PATTY

The rattling sound? Don't upset yourself. That's only rain, throwing itself against the windows. Well, the hour is late, and looks like the storm has pushed the moon to the back of the sky. I suppose it's time to speak of the choice I made some thirty years ago. Don't know why, but I feel like somebody tied a rawhide string round the roof of my skull. Could be, Mag, could be. Maybe the telling will ease off the pain.

This last portrait should help explain it all. Rafe never could argue outright with Peale, but he found other ways to defy him. Patty McGlathery was a robust Irish colleen, with hair as long as your mama's. Excepting her locks were chestnut, and Mariah's were auburn. Rafe painted this portrait of Patty in 1794, the year before the president's sitting.

After the Washington situation, Rafe started making eyes at her again, though Peale had disliked the poor girl and her family from the start. He made it clear he didn't truckle much with the Irish.

They were vulgar, blarney-mouthed folks, he said, and Patty's father was a mere house carpenter.

But in May 1797, Rafe married Patty, anyway, going straight against his pa's wishes. That's the way it was between those two. Peale stomping down his oldest child and Rafe springing back, one way or t'other.

The newlyweds settled down in a rented house on Shippin Street. Then in October of 1798, Peale put Rafe completely in charge of stuffing large animals for the museum. This meant Rafe was with the arsenic full-time. But he didn't stint the work at all. He spent hours in the preserving room with his hands in the poison water, breathing in fumes and dust.

One morning in early November, I came upstairs to sweep and overheard Peale talking to Betsy at breakfast.

"Patty sent word that Raphaelle is indisposed." Charley stabbed a slice of bacon and cracked a boiled egg. "He is suffering from chills and delirium and will not be in the museum today."

Peale sounded worried, more for his animal skins than for Rafe, I suspect. I glared at him as I pushed the hog-bristle broom across the floor. Maybe this was Peale's way of stomping Rafe again. Maybe it was time for another look at his papers.

Two days later, on November fifth, I stole a peek at his diary. Plain as day, Charley described the "numbness, convulsions, and paralytic complaints, which are the constant effects of Poison."

Sounded like Rafe's symptoms to me! If I were a judge I'd hang you, Charley Peale, I thought, when I read the words. Swing you from a gallows for poisoning Rafe!

Forgive me, Mag, but you're still a trustful yearling. You think Peale didn't have a full knowing of what he was doing. Maybe not. After all, Charley was in the habit of lying to himself. It was just in him and couldn't be taken out.

But I say he planned to misuse Rafe for the museum, same as he used me. He'd save his own self from the poison, by-the-by. If I had larruped the hide off'n Rafe with my own two hands, I wouldn't have felt worse. But I had no choice. Though Peale's papers held the secret to Rafe's health, it wasn't mine to give away. Peale still held my freedom—and Ma's rent money—in his hands.

That's the day I buried my responsibility for my friend for good. I've wished evermore I didn't have to, but if Rafe didn't care, what could I do? It's hard giving up on people, specially when they need you.

THE BIRD CASES

T ake a look at these birds here by the Mammoth Room, Mag. They remind me of something Pa used to say.

"White folks want the moon with a fence around it," he told me when I was growing up. I was most too little to understand his words at first, but they came back to me in the spring of 1799.

Old Charley strode out to the bear house one day. Spectacles balanced on his forehead and eyeballs full of purpose. I'd been making my rake talk to the straw and was well into a hard sweat.

"Moses, my man," he announced, "I am gratified that the museum is growing so quickly. Now I shall need an assistant, not just a stable boy."

"Yessir," I replied, pertish. Finally, I thought, Peale is going to free me and pay me for my labor! "I'm ready for that kind of work, Mr. Peale!"

"It's time you learned taxidermy. How to dress beach birds and place them in a natural attitude. We'll be leaving for the New Jersey Shore next week."

Plenty of folks were strolling round the walled

yard. Pairs of ladies, their open parasols like pies on a stick, little boys playing with dogs. They all disappeared as Charley's words plunged me into an all-alone place.

I knew what the trip would mean. This was no little-boy jaunt to watch Peale skin fish. This was the genuine thing. Now twould be *my* hands in the poison water—and the hands of a slave, still.

Well, I said to myself, since Peale has plans for me, I'll make some, too. The following week I packed his chest with five guns, including a rifle. Into mine I stashed heavy gloves, an extra neck scarf, and a bottle of brandy—just a little something to keep my strength up, you understand.

Early on the thirtieth, we set sail for Cape May, heading down the Delaware. It was my first time on a boat, and I liked it well enough, specially the *frump! frump!* of the wind in the sails. I remember best the laughing gulls skimming the waves. I longed to go with them. To soar away from Peale and his poison as fast as the wind would take me.

We were one day a'going, and at eleven the next morning, the shallop dropped anchor offshore. Peale rented rooms for our nightly lodging and found us a hunting shack to work in during the day.

Wasn't easy to fool him, though I managed to pass the first twenty-four hours in safety. In the early hours, I hung shelves. For the balance of the morning we shot shorebirds—summer redbirds and crested flycatchers, as I recall—and stored them on the shelves to keep rats away.

Late that afternoon Peale mixed a potion of arsenical water. I kept myself busy on t'other side of the room, away from the fumes. A breeze blew steady through the latticed windows, and I gulped fresh air like rain after a drought.

After I fashioned a table from two barrels and a door, Peale laid a tiny sanderling upon it. He carefully showed me how to gut the bird and coat its skin with arsenic.

"We must be certain to remove the meat from the thighs," he instructed, "otherwise the rotted flesh will render them useless. Furthermore, the pinions of the wings must be scraped clean."

I asked a lot of questions, so many that Peale complimented me on my curiosity. But every question required an answer, you see, and there was nothing know-all Charley Peale liked more than telling people what to do. By bedtime he had done most of the work, and I had avoided the poison. Wasn't going to be any delirium or puking for me, not that night.

Then things got trickier. Peale expected me to brew up the solution each day, which I did. I wore the neck scarves just for this purpose. Tied them round my neck, then pulled them up over my mouth and nose while I stirred the nasty soup.

I still breathed in some fumes, so I slipped outside as often as I could, pleading the need to relieve myself in the bushes. Wasn't a lie, neither, not with the brandy I sipped for courage.

The gloves? That was the easy part. When

Peale went hunting, he usually left me behind to gut and stuff the birds. I did my job as told, all right, but put on gloves to dip each carcass. They helped some, Mag, they surely did, though after a while the arsenical water soaked clear through and my fingers did get sore. Soon as I heard Peale's boots slithering back through the marshy grass, I jerked off'n the gloves and quick slipped them under my travel chest.

As far as Peale was concerned, I was as good a worker as he'd seen in his life. He told me so himself on the trip home two weeks later. We were sitting aft on a bench in the shallop. Twas a blazing hot day, and the sun made my head feel like the lid of a stove.

"You have acquired a considerable good handling of the birds, Moses," Charley said. He shaded his eyes to follow a gull's flight across the heartless blue sky.

"I enjoy working with my hands, Mr. Peale. I can do other things, too. Help Titian mount butterflies, maybe, or print labels for your displays."

Charley shook his head. "I am counting on you to take the labor of the birds from me. Raphaelle is preserving the larger animals. With you to mount the smaller ones, I will have more time to write my museum catalog."

The museum catalog was Peale's master list of his collection. Written proof of his big doings over the year. The museum meant everything to him—money, fame, respect. Like the sun that day, they all shone too bright for Mr. Charley Peale.

Your old pa was fresh out of ideas to avoid the poison. I had only one hope—Peale killed fish and birds in spring, summer, and fall. In these warm seasons, I could work outside in the museum yard. Breathe fresh air and use my gloves at the same time. Kill two birds with one stone? You could say that, Mag, indeed you could, but this was a fine kettle of fish and no joking matter at all.

Part III: EXIT

MAMMOTH ROOM

Feeling lost? Trust me, daughter, I know the way out. We'll loop through here, then head back the way we came. But I might as well warn you. When we turn right, you'll spy a monster the likes of which you've never seen before. The shadows on the wall will make the thing look twice as big as it truly is. Eleven feet high at the shoulder, fifteen feet from chin to rump—not counting the tusks, a'course. They add another eleven feet.

No, we can't skip this room. You need to know when my hatred of Peale finally sharpened to a keen point. I've never known you to be so quiet, girl. Would you like to take my hand? Didn't think so. Stick close by, then, till your eyes get used to the creature.

In the summer of 1801, Peale heard that a New York farmer had found some huge bones in a clay pit. I hadn't seen him so excited since the moving pictures show. He was thinking the bones belonged to a ten-thousand-year-old elephant. If he could reassemble them in the museum, he said, he'd never have to worry about money again.

Plus, he was annoyed with a French scientist. The man claimed American animals were puny compared to European critters. The mammoth was Peale's great chance to prove him wrong, once and for all. Had a bone to pick with the Frenchman? You might could say that, Maggie, if you were feeling clever.

Peale dropped everything. He traveled pert on a stage to New York, then boated up the Hudson to the farm. No, I didn't go along, not hardly. Don't you know, Rembrandt wormed his way into Peale's plans? Peale told Rafe and me to stay home and do our usual jobs. Took only Rembrandt with him.

That didn't stop Charley from painting us into a picture of the dig five years later. This one hanging amongst the snake skins on the back wall. Peale is on the right, his arm spread out and looking bossy as the night he freed Ma and Pa. Charley's wife is next to him, then Rembrandt's wife.

That's Rembrandt in the middle and Rubens to the right in a hat. Rafe is beside Rubens. Sophy and her husband are standing under the parasol. Why, I never noticed till you pointed it out! Peale left Rafe's wife, Patty, plumb out of the picture.

The worker turning the crank to the left of Peale is your pa. The one with sturdy legs and a strong back. Yes, you could say Peale painted me as his right-hand man, though I wasn't at the dig at all.

It was a dangerous operation, as you can see.

Peale hired men to walk the rim of the Chinese waterwheel that lifted buckets of water from the hole. Men in the pit uncovered the bones and hauled them up with ox chains. One time the sides of the crater gave way. Everybody had to scramble out before the whole contraption fell upon them.

The men were two months at work. Peale came home with empty pockets but proud of his jumble of bones, and I helped unpack the wagonload of crates. Lugged in legs, pieces of a jaw, a couple of thighbones, teeth, even a toe, all heavy as rocks. Carrying the bones was hard enough. Making sense of them was something else.

If you'll look at Rembrandt's sketch of the mammoth, you can follow me better. Peale first spread out the bones on the floor before mounting them. He put the leg bones together with hinged joints, then passed a bar of iron through the ribs to make a spine.

But the skull was all broken up. For three months in the fall of 1801, Peale and Rembrandt played with the pieces. Put them every whichaway, yet couldn't make left or right of them. I could tell Charley was getting frustrated when he let museum visitors give him advice. Of course, he didn't take any of it.

"People who think they have great knowledge," Peale sniffed, "should not be so hasty to speak."

One morning I was sweeping around the room and started fooling with the bones myself. Folks were watching me like a parcel of buzzards setting on a rail fence. I didn't pay them any mind. As I worked, I could hear scraps of talk.

"A slave wouldn't know how . . ."

"Untutored . . ."

I don't know why I took to it so easy, Mag. I wasn't trained up for that particular work, but maybe the practice with head-drawing helped me out. Anyhow, I put the fractured bones together in ways nobody had tried. Before long, they fit tight as a baked lark in a pattypan, though a few pieces were missing altogether.

Peale loved that skeleton more'n his own dog, on account of the money 'twould bring in. "I am most impressed with your work, Moses," he said when I was done. Even Rembrandt seemed excited. No, girl, he never showed it to my face. Peale introduced me to the lookers-on and bragged on me heavy.

"Ladies and gentlemen," he announced, "my servant has fitted the pieces together by trying improbable positions. The most expert anatomist could not have accomplished the fitting any better than Moses, who has the least knowledge."

The compliment meant nothing, since it was left-handed praise. But I was pleased when Rafe came down to the kitchen later to congratulate me. He looked pale as paper.

"Well done, Moze!" Rafe said with his big half-dollar smile. "Your success this morning comes at an opportune time. I have spoken to Father and urged him once again to reconsider."

"Reconsider?"

Rafe had trouble catching his breath. "In August you turned twenty-five, and every year around your birthday, I beg Father to set you free before you turn twenty-eight. This time he said he would give it serious thought. You could be a free man soon, Moze!"

I'd no idea Rafe had been pushing Peale all along for my release. Freedom three years early! I'd given up hope long ago. Still, distrustful as I was, the thought made me wild.

"Let's have a drap of whiskey and water to celebrate, Rafe!"

"I can't join you now. Father has a leopard he wants dipped."

When Rafe shuck my hand good-bye, it was

easy to tell his fingers were trembling. He wasn't free of the poison or Peale, and, I had to remember, neither was I. A wave of regret rushed over me as I held that shaky hand in my own.

Should have known not to expect much from Charley. As usual, he didn't heed Rafe at all. By December of that year, Peale had said not a word about turning me loose. When the mammoth exhibition opened on Christmas Day, I decided to butt heads with him about my freedom.

He was standing under the skeleton, and I stepped inside. There was plenty of room to spare—as you can see, the space could hold a dozen men.

"I need a minute of your time, Mr. Peale."

Charley fiddled with pieces of skull he'd fashioned from paper and glue.

"Fetch a tube of vermilion, Moses. A thin red line will indicate the division between real bone and papier-mâché. And bring a sable brush."

"Back in August you told Rafe you might set me free early."

Charley looked at me like I'd lost my wits. "This is an important opportunity for you, my man! You shall be part of the largest event in American scientific history. Haven't you heard about the local baker's mammoth loaf of bread? The thousand-pound cheese sent from Massachusetts? Why, a gentleman in Washington claims to be a 'mammoth eater.' He ate forty-two eggs in ten minutes!"

Then Peale turned back to his skull—you're

right, Mag, my skull. So the answer was no. I chomped down hard on the iron bit of slavery that December morning, but there was more humiliation to come. A week later, Charley dressed me in a feathered Indian robe and headdress. Had me ride a horse round the neighborhood. A trumpeter led the way while I handed out broadsides to people on the street.

"This enormous quadruped," said the handbill, "is the largest of terrestrial beings!" Folks followed me like goslings to Philosophical Hall, and when Peale flung open the doors, he sold a mess of tickets.

That night in the kitchen, I ripped off the headdress. Three years left till I turned twenty-eight. And when they were up, I hoped Peale would go down to hell faster'n a barrel full of nails.

Have you ever seen a coffin painted with lampblack, girl? That's how dark my life looked after the door to freedom had clanged shut again. I didn't know what a smile was from one day to the next. If only I could have seen ahead to the end of 1802, I wouldn't have suffered so.

LONG ROOM—
WINDOW SIDE

Walk with me back through the Long Room, Mag. Past the windows and down to the corner by the stove. It seems a far piece to these old eyes, but if you take my arm and we go slow, we can make it together. No, we can't light the chandelier lamps, not tonight. I expect you'll find this part of the story bright enough.

Business at the museum swole up right after January. Peale set a mouse skeleton underneath the "great carnivorous elephant of the North" to show the difference twixt the two. When visitors crowded in to see it, he raised the price of a yearly ticket to five dollars.

By March the museum had bust its walls again. Peale had another slippery talk with the government folks. Asked could he rent the second floor and tower rooms of the State House. The State House is the third home of Peale's Museum—the very building we're standing in now, and pictured in this engraving resting on the exhibit case. It's here that they signed the Declaration of Independence and

BACK OF THE STATE HOUSE, PHILADELPHIA

wrote the Constitution. Left slaves out of the deal, but this is taking me away from my tale.

Thanks to the mammoth, Peale was living in high fashion. Betsy had been hankering for a cook maid, someone to help with the care of the four babes she'd borne since marrying Charley. He was sitting so pretty, he bought an indenture for an orphan girl, and that's how I first met your ma.

She arrived at Philosophical Hall in early spring 1802. It was one of those perfumy days when the trees are filling out with a pale green lace. Betsy showed her to her closet of a room, then brought her to the kitchen. I was sitting at the table, tearing into my midday meal of bread and dried herring.

"Take some refreshment, Mariah," said Betsy. She waved her pudgy hand toward to the table. "Later I'll introduce you to the youngest children—Linnaeus, Benjamin Franklin, Sybilla, and Titian Ramsay."

Next to the portly Betsy, your ma looked like a young sapling tree. "Yes, Mum," she said, her big brown eyes glued upon me.

"A pot of water is simmering over the fire. Moses will show you where the tea is kept. I'll return in a quarter of an hour."

But when Betsy made to leave, Mariah burst into tears. Bleated like a calf who's slipped through a hole in the fence, and the mama's too big to come after her.

"Here now," I said, gruffer than I meant to be, but a weeping woman will do that to a man, "I'll make the tea, miss, if that's what's fretting you."

As I rose from the bench, Mariah ran from the room. Betsy followed her with an impatient swish of skirts, leaving me to stare at my plate and wonder if I'd ever be hungry again.

Well, you might think my feed's been off lately, Mag, but it only appears that way, as you'll eat anything that doesn't fall out of your mouth.

Anyhow, twasn't that Mariah didn't like colored people. She just wasn't accustomed to the mix of skins on Philadelphia's streets. The fox-grape sheen of slaves from Santo Domingo, the ginger cake runaways from the South.

Your ma was only sixteen. Fresh off the boat

from Ireland, orphaned, and deep homesick for the cool, green hills of that land. When she saw my brown face, she told me later, all the strangeness of this new place washed over her.

I finally did get Mariah to sit at the table with me, or you wouldn't be here to hear the story. But my heart got most wore out before it happened. After that first go-out, Mariah got a bit used to me. Had to, as I ate three meals a day with her in the kitchen. I had a dickens of a time getting a word out of her, though. Found out later she could hardly understand us flat-talking Americans.

"Let me put some wood on the fire for you," I'd offer, trying in my fumbly way to start a conversation. Only answer I got was a paltry smile.

"Do you need some water from the pump?" I'd ask, and she'd hum a pretty Irish tune in reply. Seemed like the ice between us was thick as an Irish ha'penny.

Still, your ma had a sweet air that left me feeling good and walking real light. Cheered me up just to be round her. Specially when Peale started hunting birds again, and I had to stir poison in the yard.

One time she brought a slice of fresh soady bread out to me. Her bread was something good, wasn't it, Mag? Shot through with currants and so light, it crumbled like cake in your mouth. Made me forget I was working with the poison, and calmed the stomach cramps I got a time or two.

After summer passed, we were still only halfway to friendly. But on Christmas Day 1802, the chill started coming off, and this is how it came about.

I figured Mariah didn't have many dainties. After her folks died, she'd been packed off to America by cousins as poor as she was. Had no more than a beggar's share in her valise, most likely, when she arrived on these shores.

So I bought a needle case from a seamstress down at the market. It was a showy thing embroidered with vines and leaves. Inside was a flannel leaf for needles and a pocket for thimble and pins. I wrapped it in the red cloth from Pa's wooden box, tied it with twine, and left it sitting on the table for your ma to find on Christmas morning. Then I made myself scarce.

After Mariah had fixed a holiday breakfast for the Peales, I came back to the kitchen. Found her taking off her apron and tying the frayed ribbons of a black bonnet under her chin.

"Yer looking good for yourself, Mr. Williams," she said, her eyes bright. "Thank ye for the gift. And will ye be going to church this Christmas morning?"

"No," I answered before thinking.

I'd never been much of a churchgoer. Gone once or twice when Ma got after me hot, just to ease her off from getting into a lot of meanness, but suddenly church seemed like the smart place to be.

"Not by myself, that is," I said, startled by my own words. "I'm meeting Ma up at St. George's."

Mariah smiled with approval. "Ah, 'tis a lovely

thing entirely to celebrate Christ's birthday with your murther."

Her brogue was thick as mutton stew. "God bless ye both, and I'll say a prayer for ye at Mass."

I couldn't figure out why Ma and I needed praying over, but anything Mariah wanted to offer, I would accept. Yes, I did meet your granny at church that Christmas morning. I didn't go out looking any kinda way. Tidied up and put on my best. Ma said I looked fit to kill when I showed up in one of Rafe's top hats and a new muslin shirt. It was a fine holiday, and three days later, I got the best gift of all—a physiognotrace.

LONG ROOM—
NORTHWEST CORNER

Make us a little fire in the stove, girl, while I fold some banknote paper for the machine. I know it's a hard word to say. Listen to me, then you try it. Fizz-ee-og-no-trace.

On December 28, 1802, Peale bought the rights to use this invention from a fellow named Hawkins. Charley installed the device here in the corner and screwed it tight to the wall. It's a good thing, as it was used heavy from the start.

Folks who couldn't afford an oil portrait were eager to hand over one penny to make their own profile. Quakers liked the shadow pictures, too, since the simple black image was more fitting to their plain way of life.

The fire feels good to my hands, Mag. They been sore some lately, and I need to warm them before tracing your face. Now, you have a seat in the chair. That's it, just under the machine, with your head to the side of it. I'll lower the board in the middle till the scooped-out part fits snug on your shoulder. Rest the side of your chin in the little cup and hold still.

I know you can't see what's going on! If you want to follow along, look at the watercolor Peale painted of the physiognotrace. It's straight ahead of you, hanging on the end wall.

See the square contraption in the picture? The thing with movable joints? Poking out from the bottom is a brass pin. I'm going to guide the pin round your face, head, and neck, like so.

Notice the stylus at the top? It's making an indentation on the folded paper just beneath it. Quit your wiggling—can't help if it tickles. We're almost done. Now, I'll just remove the folded paper, and here's a miniature outline of my Maggie's lovable face! Since I folded the paper twice, you'll have four hollow cutouts soon—each one exactly the same.

Hand me the scissors sitting on the ream of paper. This next step is a tricky one. No, you can't help, but you can listen while I cut. Let you try? I don't know . . . we'll see, we'll see.

After hearing about the physiognotrace, customers poured into the museum. Whole families at a time. Peale kept a turnstile at the bottom of the steps. He attached a bell so's he could hear people coming up, and that bell sang like a mockingbird.

One day in early January, I was up here at the end of the Long Room, arranging a bird in a case. I started watching a woman cut a profile of her child, and this is when I got another idea for getting to know your ma. Soon as dusk settled that evening, I went to the kitchen.

"Will you come with me, miss?" I asked.

Mariah looked puzzled, but she threw on a shawl, and I led her down the short gravel path over to the State House. Twas a foul night much like tonight, and about this time of year. She was balky at first.

"And where will ye be taking me, Mr. Williams?" she asked. I didn't answer, as the wind was too nippy to stand and argue. Brought her up the same broad stairs you climbed tonight, Mag, and settled her in the chair you're sitting in now.

Then I passed the brass rod round her face and head. She blushed when I brushed her cheek, but I wasn't aiming to court her, just talk to her. Now, girl, you're flustering me! Well, her skin was soft as starlight, if you have to know.

That's why the first time I cut the folded paper,

my hands shook a bit. I made her nose too short and had to take another tracing. Finally I cut one that exactly matched her features. I placed it on a pasteboard covered with black paper, tacked it into one of Peale's gilt frames, and handed it to her.

I can picture Mariah now, if I close my eyes. She stared at her profile for the longest time, as if she'd never noticed her long eyelashes or the topknot of curls on her head. A looking glass can tell the whole story of a face, yet can't hold it for long. A shadow picture tells only half the tale, but keeps it forever.

"Sure, and it's a cunning thing!" she cried. "Is it my true likeness?" I held the profile beside her head and studied it with a sharp eye.

"It's you, all right, miss, though you're a heap prettier than the picture shows." As soon as I said the words, I wished I could eat them out of the air. I'd just got her talking to me. Now I was being too forward!

"May I send two to my cousins in County Mayo, and keep one for myself?"

"Why, a'course!" I was relieved she didn't mind me calling her pretty, and pleased she fancied my handiwork enough to send it way across the grandywater.

"What about the fourth copy?"

"Would you like to have it, Mr. Williams?" Mariah gave me a playful smile. I do admit I wanted to lay a kiss on her then and there, but I held back. Something told me I better go slow with her.

And so I did. During the winter of 1803, we

passed many a friendly evening in the kitchen. While she mended, I read some of her favorite texties aloud from the Bible, her needle case sitting on the table between us like a silent secret. Sometimes I helped her clean the heavy kittles, and we'd gripe about Peale's pig litter of a family. Or we worked in peaceable silence while she whistled one of her rolling Irish tunes.

"What's that lively song, miss?" I asked one night.

The old bashfulness sprang up again. "Aye, I can tell ye the name, but not the words," she answered softly. "'Tis called 'Do You Love an Apple, Do You Love a Pear?'"

Made not a lick of sense, but then, many of your ma's Irish ways confounded me. She drank tea so strong, I could have ridden it round the kitchen. And any little skeer, she'd make a sign of the cross in front of her face.

It was that night I made up my mind. Mariah was the one I wanted, and from then on, I never yearned to make any swaps. I suspected she felt the same way, though I couldn't ask her to marry me outright.

I'll tell you why not. There were a good number of mixed couples in Philadelphia by then. The 1780 manumission law had dropped the old ban on slaves and whites loving and living together. Still, I didn't want your ma getting hooked to a husband who was bound to another man.

A year and a half till I turned twenty-eight, and

Peale might turn me loose. It was time for another plan. I didn't know how much Charley would want, but no matter the price, somehow I'd buy myself free.

LONG ROOM—
NORTHWEST END

The very next day, Peale and I were working here at the end of the Long Room. He was in a rosy mood, and you can guess why—Sophy was in the ticket office, filling the cash drawer with a steady flow of bright quarters. While I held a white crane by the tippy ends of its feathers, Peale stuck a painted seascape in the back of a case.

I lit into it straight off. "Mr. Peale, I know a way you can triple your money." Peale's pointy ears seemed to twitch at the sound of the word.

"And what might that be?"

"Let me run the physiognotrace. Most people have no trouble passing the rod around their face. But a good many can't do the cutting. End up with noses and chins they've not been born with. I can do a better job of it, and folks are vain enough to pay more for a true likeness."

"How much more?"

"Well, ten cents sounds too high—that's almost half the price of an admission ticket. Five cents is too low, as people suspect they only get what they pay for." I could almost hear the pennies clinking in Peale's mind.

"Eight cents would be about right. I would keep five." I stuck this in the middle of my speech, Maggie, so Peale wouldn't dwell on it too long.

"The museum would take the other three cents," I said quickly. "That's a two-hundred-per-cent profit over the one penny you charge now!"

Peale's face took on the crafty look I'd seen so many times before. I expected the idea to appeal to him. Twould add a sizable amount to money he made from his one-dollar frames.

"Your idea holds merit, Moses, although I'd like to see a sample of your work before I agree. But who would preserve my birds when spring arrives? Last year you barely kept pace with the large numbers that arrived daily."

It never struck me till that moment. If I shirked the poison pot outside, it might mean more hours inside the preserving room for Rafe. Rafe, who wouldn't avoid fumes or dust. The thought entered the front door of my mind, then slipped out the back before I could stop it.

"Let me make profiles of you and Mrs. Peale," I offered. "If you like them, I'll try the machine with the customers for a day or two."

My plan worked better than I ever thought it would. That night I took the Peales' shadow pictures. Did them up right, showing Charley's strong nose and even the knot in his neck scarf.

Betsy's abundant bosom turned out nicely, as

did her squishy starched cap. I'll admit I trimmed her pleated double chin a bit and gave her a daintier nose. Wouldn't hurt, I figured, to make the lady of the house prettier than she really was.

Peale let me start here in the corner the next day. Within a week, folks were lined up clear into the Quadruped Room, waiting to pay eight cents for a flattering picture. Before long, I was better'n belly deep in paper heads left over from the hollow-cut profiles.

Peale brought in two barrels, and every so often, I gathered the heads up and threw them in. "Blockheads" he called them, when he got irritated at customers who stood on the upholstered benches or left prints on the glass cases.

Charley had me stamp every profile with the words PEALE'S MUSEUM. No, ma'am, my name was nowhere in sight. He did list me in his *Guide to the Philadelphia Museum*, though I didn't get a name there, either.

"The Attendant is allowed to receive 8 cents for cutting out each set of profiles," Peale wrote, "from such as choose to employ him."

Struck me the same way. I'd lived twenty-six years with Charley and worked for him all that time. Yet I was still just the man in the corner, an "attendant" with no name.

Things drifted along like that for a spell, with the money pouring in. Yet by spring I hadn't seen my share, and freedom looked no nearer than dawn does at midnight. That same summer, Rafe got in the act. When he saw how successful I was, he made his own physiognotrace. It was against the law to copy Hawkins's machine, but Rafe didn't care a whit. He carted it around to towns and plantations all over Virginia.

I'll tell you how I felt about him cutting profiles. Twas the same old two-way setup. I was relieved, as any work he did outside the museum meant less time with the poison.

But I almost hated him for it, too. Seemed like he had taken over the one thing I could call my own. He could travel willy-nilly with his physiognotrace, and got to keep all the profits to boot.

When Rafe came back in September, he stopped in the corner for a visit. I noticed right off that his hands were steady and his color was fresh. Hadn't seen him looking so good since . . . well, since before the poison.

He pulled up one of the upholstered benches and straddled it. Looked carefree as a boy out of school, though he was a grown man of twenty-nine.

"The face-i-o-trace has done well by me, Moze," he said, puffy with pride. I smiled at Rafe's word joke in spite of myself. "I cut thousands of vellum paper profiles down in Virginia!"

"That's a mighty high number," I agreed. As I made a stack of the folded paper, I felt the old carbuncle of envy coming to a head again.

"How much did you charge?"

"Twenty-five cents for four profiles. Ten dollars to paint them in watercolor. People in

Richmond went wild over them, and the citizens of Norfolk overflowed my rooms! They couldn't resist the advertisement."

Rafe pulled a scrap of newspaper out of his pocket, then clambered upon the bench.

"DEATH," he read in a deep voice, "deprives us of our friends, and then we regret having neglected the opportunity of obtaining their likeness."

I had to chuckle again at the way Rafe said the clever words. He was as good as his pa at fishing for publicity. But twenty-five cents for four shadow pictures! Ten dollars for a painted one. While I was stuck here in the corner, working for a nickel per set.

"And I included a guarantee for doubters," Rafe crowed. "No likeness, no pay!"

"Miss Patty will sure enough be glad to have you home with full pockets." I whet my scissors on an oiled stone. "How much did you pull in?"

"Sixteen hundred dollars," he told me right off. "Enough to make a deposit on a house on Powell Street." I knew Patty had been stomping her foot for a new-built home. Rafe sounded relieved to get her off his back, and had everything else been equal, I'd have been happy for him. Instead, with Mariah's face floating in my mind, I begged for help.

"Mr. Peale agreed to pay me five cents a cutting, Rafe, yet I've seen not a penny. Since he is determined to keep me, I'd like to put the money toward my free papers. I'd be obliged if you'd speak to him."

Rafe's face drooped like the feathers on a slayed bird. "I'll assist you any way I can, Moze. You know I have tried, but when it comes to you and money, Father follows his own nose."

Then he brightened. "Let me treat you to a nip at the Black Bear!"

In those days, Mag, I liked my suds as well as the next man. Yet even I knew Rafe spent too much time looking down the whiskey glass. Anyway, I couldn't leave my post. Not while there was money to be made. The bell on the turnstile rang downstairs.

"Customers coming, Rafe. I better stay in the corner."

And that's where I sat, with nothing to count except lost hopes and the months till I turned twenty-eight.

QUADRUPED ROOM

Let's wind back through the Quadruped Room, and I'll tell you what happened the afternoon of January 1, 1804. Remember the date well, girl.

When Peale came down the steps, Mariah was washing dishes and I was cutting eyes from potatoes. Seeing him made me recall the evening so long ago when he set Ma and Pa free.

Almost eighteen years had passed. Peale was an old man of sixty-three. Still siring babes and had one on the way, overdue by a month. But now his head was bald as the white eagle he kept in the yard, and his blue eyes had faded to gray.

I was surprised to see Rafe behind Peale. He stepped forward and clasped my hand. "We've brought you some welcome news, Moze," he said, glancing at his pa.

Peale hesitated, then spoke. "In order to close out my accounts for the year, I counted the heads in the barrels, Moses. You cut eight thousand eight hundred profiles in 1803. That's an average of almost twenty-five per day."

"I knew I'd been going at a fast pace," I replied. And where is my money? I wondered.

"Here is your share of the profit," Charley mumbled, looking kinda lukewarm as he slowly counted out four hundred and fifty dollars in cash. He laid the new green bills in my hand, each the color of a shiny katydid.

"Yes, and himself has earned it entirely!" Mariah said hotly. The way she burred her r's made the words ripple like pianny music.

Peale looked put out with my darling heart, but I knew where her bile came from. Mariah toiled for room, board, and a few pennies a week. Almost the same as being a slave.

"Father has something else to tell you, Moses." Rafe looked hard at his daddy, pushing him to say the words.

"Our agreement was to free you at twenty-eight." Agreement! Was there a bottom to the pot of Peale's lies?

"I would have done sooner, of course, but for worry that you would loiter about the streets."

For a long moment I craved the feel of his flesh against my fist, but I wouldn't hit him, not in front of your ma.

The man like to talked me to death before getting to the point. "I feel confident that the physiognotrace, like the mammoth, will give good milk in years to come. Since you have learned the skill so well, Raphaelle has urged me to make a free man of you. As of today."

I wanted to remind him it was my profile-cutting what gave good milk, but I hoped to work in the museum for years to come. Wasn't any use to arguing, not if I wanted to keep my job.

"Thank you, Mr. Peale," I replied, though why I should be thanking him for myself, I did not know. "Do you think we can make a weekly arrangement for my share of the profile money? So's I can start paying Ma's rent myself?"

"Father will settle with you every Saturday evening," Rafe said firmly, "before he makes his deposit in the Bank of North America. And he will register your manumission papers at the Pennsylvania Abolition Society. There will be no mistake about your free status."

So Rafe had done it at last. For once he had wrestled Charley's strong will to the ground...not for his own sake, but for mine. I was proud of Rafe, because only I understood the struggle between those two. We shuck hands all around, then your ma offered to make tea.

"Thank you, no, Mariah," said Peale, all business and bustle. "Raphaelle is in the midst of preserving a shipment of African birds."

Off they went up the steps, me trailing behind them like a sorry-looking lost sheep. Mariah touched my arm, holding me back till they were gone.

"You're free, Mr. Williams," she said quietly. "Peale has his sons to help him now."

I felt foolish, forgetting myself like that, but I

needed to hear the words before I could believe them: *I was free*.

"Settle down at the table," she said, "and we'll have our tea. Then you can walk to Elbow Lane and tell your mother the wondrous news! With you to pay her rent, she's finally free of Peale, too."

As Mariah set the pot to boil, she hummed the Irish tune she loved so well. Only this time she started singing the words.

Well, they went something like this, Mag, though you've got to promise not to laugh at my scratchy voice:

> DO YOU LOVE AN APPLE?
> DO YOU LOVE A PEAR?

And before I knew it, Mariah was holding my hands. Whispering the rest of the words in my ear:

> DO YOU LOVE A LADDY WITH CURLY
>   BROWN HAIR?
> AH, YES, I LOVE HIM, I CANNOT DENY
>   HIM.
> I'LL BE WITH HIM WHEREVER HE GOES.

Now, I've made free enough with this part of the story, girl. It's enough to say your ma and I were wedded in Saint Mary's Catholic Church the next year. Peale put us down in his marry book—the big dictionary where he listed important dates.

Mariah and I, we were blessed in marriage. The itching heel never got ahold of either one of us. We had a good twenty years together, and the grandest thing is, we had two angel children. Yes, my girl, one of them was you.

PRIVACY ROOM

What did freedom feel like? I'll tell you, soon as we rest again in the lecture hall. Over this way, in the little enclosure Peale built for privacy. Yes, I can read, too, Maggie. "No admittance," says the sign on the door, but if Peale's where I think he is, he's too hot to care. Now then, where was I?

Freedom? Well, there wasn't any blowing of trumpets and banging of drums, as it didn't happen all at once. First, Mariah had to work off her indenture for Charley, then I had to save and buy us a house. Still, by 1806, we were not dependent on anyone else for tomorrow. Had a life of our own, with no rain except what falls natural into every life.

I tasted sorrow when your granny died of influenza, and it nigh burst Mariah's heart when our firstborn took with the fever. No, I didn't send for the doctor. We stuck to recipes for teas and salves your granny Lucy had taught me. Nursed little Phoebe ourselves, but lost her, anyway. Your ma cried till her apron was limp.

Times got tough after the Panic of 1819. When museum business slowed to a trickle, I went into debt. Couldn't pay the ground rent on my Walnut Street lot and sold it in 1823.

All in all, though, we had a good life, and I've known the pleasure of a job well done. Followed profile-cutting all this time. Surely every parlor in Philadelphia has one hanging in it, as I've made thousands each year.

No, not too many profiles of colored folks. Rafe took one of me before I was wed. Did a tolerable fine job, too. Showed the broad chest and good head of hair I sported back then. And here, I've a recent blockhead in my wallet. Cut it a month or two ago. Remember the woman on Elbow Lane that your granny nursed through the fever? This young fellow is her grand. Well, yes, we could stroll over there sometime so's you could meet him. Girl, you do tickle me. That shy smile on your face reminds me of your ma.

Speaking of which, after Betsy died in childbirth, my profiles helped Charley find a new wife. He met a Quaker named Hannah while I was taking her shadow picture. The two were married inside a few months. She was a gentle woman, though Peale never could break her of dipping snuff. Hannah passed in 1821, leaving Peale a widower for the third time.

I've met some interesting characters in my line of work. Cut a profile of a German baron in 1804. In 1806 I took the pictures of ten Indian chiefs.

And I remember well the fellow from North Carolina.

"I don't want a mulatto fooling with me," he complained when he spied me in the corner.

"Sir, I assure you no one can match the perfection of Moses' cutting," Peale replied.

The man finally agreed to sit, but after all the commotion, I found it distasteful to trace his face. I managed to do it without touching him and soiling myself in the process.

Top Landing

Rafe? Let's step out to the landing. I'll tell you about him. Don't hang over the railing, Mag, you're liable to turn giddy and fall. Come to think of it, the Great Stairs remind me of Rafe. While Mariah and I were moving up in life, we passed him going down. He was headed for some forlorn place and wouldn't let anybody come along.

My friend felt like he couldn't do anything right, is all I know. Compared to Rembrandt, he was a failure in the portrait business. Patty complained when Rafe made no money, but every time he traveled to cut profiles, she wanted him home to help with their four babes. When Rafe did come back to Philadelphia, he had to suck up the arsenic dust.

Unlike me. Your ma was right. My duties with the poison were over after I started in the corner. Peale did find him another assistant to help in the museum. Three, to be exact. His son Rubens, a hired fellow name of James, and Jacob, a young apprentice.

Before long, Rubens refused to work with the

poison. Said it gave him piles and indigestion. After five years, James left the museum, and Jacob, he just walked out one day. Left Charley out of sorts, losing all his help like that, and it threw the taxidermy jobs straight back on Rafe.

I often thought I should talk to Rafe about the poison again, indeed I did! Specially after he went off his head in 1806. He cut over two hundred thousand profiles down in South Carolina and sent the money home, along with birds he preserved for the museum. But something happened to his mind while he was gone. It went crooked and couldn't be put back straight.

When Rafe returned, I decided I had to caution him again about the arsenic. Not enough to cause any trouble with Peale, you understand, only a little warning. I'd been boxing with the idea ever since my slavery ended. Though it was against my wants to interfere, I figured I owed it to Rafe, since I had got my freedom early by him.

Twas one of those sticky July days that sits on you like a thick coat. The museum was near empty, so I left my corner to visit Rafe in the preserving room. He was working on a shipment of manatees from South America, twenty-eight, as I recollect.

I took a seat on a stool near the door. Didn't want to get to close too the arsenic, you see.

"How you feeling, Rafe? I hear your family's been worried about you."

Rafe looked up and frowned. "It was a disagreeable time, Moze, but I'm much improved."

He laid a red-feathered bird on the table and split it down the middle with a sharp penknife. Pulled the flesh out with a wire hook.

"What happened—was it a fever?"

He rubbed the bird skin with a bar of arsenic soap, tore the feathers, and swore under his breath. His eyes had a chased look—I'd seen the expression somewhere before but couldn't place it.

"I was cursed with a run of bad luck. First, the leaky ship almost sank on the passage down. Then a horse ran away from me, and I fractured my leg. The doctors said the problems led to ravings in my mind."

When the feathers fell apart in Rafe's hands, he swore again. "The physicians advised me to return home without delay or risk death."

He threw the sullied bird in the corner and lit into another one, trying to go easy, I could see that. But his hands were shaking so bad, I could barely stand to watch. Then I remembered. Rafe's eyes reminded me of the animals Peale raised in the yard. Right before Charley shot them, they took on the same hunted stare. Don't know how, but they always sensed something evil was on the way.

"I still think that arsenic is wicked stuff. Wear some gloves, why don't you?" I suggested.

"And tear more feathers? Gloved fingers would be too rough on these delicate skins! At any rate, I became aware of the power of arsenic while in South Carolina. My discovery there proves it beyond a doubt."

"What discovery?"

Rafe got peevish with the question. "While in Charleston," he barked impatiently, "I discovered that arsenic can preserve ship bottoms. It will kill marine worms, the same ones that cling to pilings at the wharf."

I got testy right back. "If you've seen arsenic kill worms, Rafe, then why do you work with it day after day? Still trying to satisfy your daddy?" It was spiteful of me, Maggie, but I couldn't stop myself. I was finally free of Peale! Why wouldn't Rafe shake himself loose, too?

"Father says he depends on me. There's no one else to do the taxidermy now. And he gives Patty and me pecuniary aid when we are low on funds."

Rafe's voice was hollow, like he was speaking from inside a cauldron. "There's no other way to repay him."

It was true Peale doled out money to Rafe. I'd often heard him complain about it. Though it must've hurt Charley's pocketbook, looked to me like just another way to keep his oldest on a leash. I saw then that Peale had finally won the long battle of wills.

I've got a deep chill in my bones, girl. Let's keep moving, so I can shake it off. What's wrong? You sure got a turndown mouth on you! Well, I had good reasons for not pushing Rafe harder to give up the poison.

First off, I had to keep my job. No use stirring up trouble in the Peale family when there was trouble aplenty brewing outside the museum walls. You take July 4, 1805, for instance. Whites drove free coloreds out of the Independence Day celebration down in the State House yard. I saw it with my own eyes from a window in the Mammoth Room, and the profanity liked to have scorched my ears.

That's when I joined Bethel Church. The one Richard Allen started when whites wouldn't let free blacks pray anymore at Saint George's. I've found some fine fellowship inside Mother Bethel's walls.

A number of Philadelphia coloreds were kidnapped at gunpoint around that same time. Herded aboard slavers down at the wharfs. Only thing that saved some of the free men were the white families that had emancipated them. I wasn't about to start trouble with the Peales. They were my insurance policy, and I had to keep the premiums paid.

That's why I left Rafe alone. Life was too satisfying to risk losing my income or my freedom. Anyway, when a grown man sets out to destroy himself, there's not much a body can do.

Ticket Office

Rafe didn't fall straight down to the bottom in one long slide. He flickered bright, then dim, like the whale oil street lamps down on Chestnut Street.

It's hard to know what got to him first—the poison or the drink. I'm inclined to believe the first led to the second, as the liquor must have eased his pain. He'd take a week at a time, drinking and singing. Went to skulduggery at night with ladies of loose character. Got so's the city watchmen knew him well. They often brought him home from the Black Bear Inn and dumped him on Patty's doorstep.

In 1809, he went to the hospital for two weeks. Delirium, Peale said it was, caused by excessive spirits. The worse Rafe got, the more Peale claimed he was drinking too much on the side.

But I knew the truth. Delirium was Rafe's first serious symptom of poisoning, way back in 1798. The very same, though I kept my lips closed tight about it. I wasn't going to be the one to take Charley's lies away from him.

Around 1814, right before you were born, Rafe had a bad attack. Violent stomach pains, weakness, and more delirium. According to the grapevine news, he went eight days with no stool, if you can believe it. Yet he recovered as soon as he left the preserving room. Rented a house in the country, where he painted still lifes like this one to his soul satisfaction.

Have a look-see to the right, and you'll know what I mean. I always liked this particular picture of dried herring, since it's my choice food. And here's the same blue-striped bowl Rafe favored as a boy.

I agree with you. The picture is powerful true to life, and I can almost see Rafe's smile behind the shadows. Even Peale finally had to admit the still lifes were something special. He bragged on the pictures and sent some to London to be sold.

But Rembrandt still floated on the top of his Pa's mind. Around the museum it was always, "my son Rembrandt" this, "my son Rembrandt" that. Twice Peale sent him to Paris to study art. Rembrandt swaggered like a drunken cow when he returned, certain *he* was the master artist, not Rafe. No wonder Rafe threatened to kill himself, along about 1818. Don't know why my eyes are leaking so, Maggie. Must be the smoke from the lantern.

PRESERVING ROOM

This is the last stop on our tour—the poison place. This is the workroom Peale built over the stairs back in 1802. Makes me feel old and thrown away to see these crumbling plaster walls. Pull us up two stools, so's I can finally be done with my tale. Stretch out on the table and rest? I'm old, but I'm still round here, and don't you forget it, girl.

Here's the final picture, leaning in the corner— Rafe's portrait, painted by Peale. You'll notice one thing right off. Rafe's hair is falling out on one side of his head, from the arsenic, I believe. You can't tell it from the painting, but his knuckles were so gnarly, he could hardly pick up a brush without pain. After he took with a swelling in his legs, he gave up most of the taxidermy chores.

You were well past your creeping days when things got real bad. Rafe left home for days at a time, and Patty was so poor, she tried to sell the house. She even wanted to farm the children out to relatives, as her sewing couldn't pay the food bills. Said her husband was a drunken spendthrift.

Patty had a determined disposition, yet I won't fault her for it. When Rafe's humor turned nasty, he aimed it straight at her. Once he made a fool of her, right in front of the children. Painted a piece of tin so's it looked like a pile of dog leavings. Placed his trick-of-the-eye on the carpet, then let her nag him to sweep it up. Rafe gave a wicked laugh when he told me about it, but I knew it wasn't like him to be so mean. The poison had wrecked his mind.

A cure? You've hit on something there, Maggie, but we'll get to that. After the painted tin business, I wondered what Charley was thinking. Didn't he notice how bad off his son was? Was he still lying to himself and others about the arsenic? I dipped again into his letter book one day, and came up with the proof all over my face.

On July 4, 1820, Peale warned Rafe against any medicine for his ailments. Said "all things considered, it were better for Mankind if not a particle of Medicine existed on the face of the earth!"

He closed with one last stinger. "I hope you will shine as a portrait painter—for as I have always said, if you could have confidence in yourself, and paint portraits with the same exactness of finish as you have done in still life, that no Artist could be your superior in that line."

Confidence! How could Rafe ever believe in himself? By 1824, he was making only three dollars for a watercolor profile and fifteen for an oil portrait. Might as well have given them away, as Rembrandt took in one hundred dollars for his own paintings. When money was desperate low, Rafe even stooped to raffling off his art. Put some up at auction and traded others to carpenters and bricklayers for work on his house.

Sorry, Maggie. I'll try to speak up, but I've a pain in my chest. Too much talking, I reckon. I think I will linger awhile on this table, if you'll help me up.

The last time I saw Rafe was in early March 1825. I passed him crossing Market Street as I was on my way to the museum. The morning was blustery, with dirty woolen clouds hanging from the sky.

He was shivering like a wet puppy and barely able to hobble alongside the granite curbstone. Clutched a few sheets of foolscap in his hand.

"Salutations, my friend!"

In spite of the lines of pain plowing his face, Rafe was cheerful. Sober, too, though his eyes looked like empty rooms.

"That's a steep bit of curbing, Rafe. Can I help you up?" Made my heart crack like the varnish on one of Peale's paintings, seeing Rafe in misery one way and then the other.

"Perhaps a little boost, if you will. My old enemy, the gout, has been nagging me lately. I should have listened to you, Moses. Those hours with the arsenic have left me unfit to paint."

Rafe was right, but times like that, there's nothing to say, Mag. I silently held his elbow and gave it a lift. When a piece of paper fell out of his hand, I stooped to grab it.

"What's this, Rafe? You sending love notes to some pretty gal?"

He gave a rattley chuckle. "These are couplets I've written for a candy maker, down on Market Street below Fourth. He puts them inside his confections and sells them as "secrets.""

"I always knew you were a great painter, Rafe. Had no idea you were a poet, too!" I kept my voice gay and quick, but I was low inside. Rafe could only be making pennies for his doggerel.

"Most are silly lovesick poems. The comic ones are the best of the lot. Here, I'll read one to you." Rafe began to recite, then choked on a coughing fit.

We went into the nearest store, where I found him a seat behind a six-plate woodstove. He complained of a pain in his gut, and it came to me then. Lately Rafe had been too sick to work with the arsenic, but over the years, it had dammed up in him like sludge in a drain.

I flew to the apothecary next door. Begged a tumbler of milk mixed with a teaspoon of sulfur and took it to Rafe, but he waved it away. Said he was too sick to drink it. I stayed with him for the longest, till his color came back. Then Sophy's boy, Escol, wandered into the store. Rafe promised his nephew would look after him and sent me on my way. It was poor reliance, yet what else could I do?

The next day Escol kindly brought me the news. Rafe tried to make it home alone but collapsed in the Third Street Market House. Police called a friend, who took him back to Powell Street.

Rafe never did get better. For three days he was twisted in torment—a living death, Escol said. I was relieved to hear the hurting stopped when mortification set in. Once the flesh starts to rot with gangrene, it can't feel pain.

Then my poor friend just lay down to die. His suffering ended on March 4, 1825. Less than two years ago, though it seems like two lifetimes.

I went alone to the burying at Saint Peter's, because your ma was coughing too hard to go out in the rain. That's right, that's right, Mag, I had lost the memory—you sat with her while I was gone.

It was a weepy scene. The watery sky had darkened the headstones and turned the ground to muck. Patty and the children—four boys and three girls by then—huddled under the bare branches of an Osage orange tree. Mourning the wasted life of the man as well as his death, I suspect.

Though Peale had little to say to Patty after the service, he spoke freely to his friends. Wiped his eyes as he walked the winding path from the cemetery to the street. "My son was in great suffering," he said, "yet he died happy and content."

When I heard Peale's next words, seemed like the rain should turn to blood. Should run down to red up the earth over Rafe's wooden coffin. "Raphaelle was perfectly resigned to his fate," murmured Charley, and for once, he told the truth.

Folks still say Rafe died of the whiskey fits, but that's according to Peale. I say Peale let die one of the best people ever to put a shoe on. Rafe had a generous heart and never did harm to any man. Sometimes I think I'm as bad as Ma—I can hear him calling me, begging for sulfur and milk.

When he left, a part of me left, too. And I know who really killed him. Don't ever clasp a secret too close to your heart, Mag. It clings like a moth at first, quiet and still, then flails about every whichaways. A secret will devil you to death, so I'm letting mine fly free.

I locked it away when I copied pages from Peale's diaries twixt 1788 and 1790. Hid it again when I peeped at his autobiography. If only I'd spoken sooner, Rafe might be smiling with us today.

What are you doing, girl, fooling with my head? Why, that's only a bald patch from wearing a top hat too many years. I guess my hair is getting as thin as these spindle-legs.

Arsenic poisoning? Not hardly, Mag. If twas going to get me, wouldn't I know by now?

Listen well, Maggie. I want you to learn the end of the tale, but I'm too tired to finish now. Look in my vest pocket. This is where I always keep the key to Pa's box. If something should ever happen—now don't get blubbery, I'm not leaving anytime soon— find this key before they ease me in the ground.

You'll find Pa's box in my bottom bureau drawer, along with a list of the contents. Be sure to tick it off, and make sure nothing's missing. You won't see rubies or gold. Just a few whatnots that are treasures only to me. Like the pages I copied from Peale's papers so long ago. Look careful at the underlined words. They'll show the crime I been wanting to confess all night. In the box you'll also find the deed to the house and a little cash. You might need both sometime. Decide to marry, maybe, or start your own business. A profile cutting shop? That would please me, it surely would.

One more thing. Some folks think because they are wise in books, they are wise in all things. Well, education is one thing, and I'm glad you're getting yours. But fireside training is another.

I've reared you to puzzle out life's problems on your own. Now you got to go make your mark in the world and decide who to help on the way. You've got a big heart, girl, and I'm proud of it, but sometime you'll have to choose, too. Measure how much of another's pain you're able to bear.

Just remember one thing when you read Peale's papers. It doesn't matter if the helping makes a difference. It's the trying that counts.

Maybe it'll be easier for you than it's been for me. My slavery days, they were dog days. Peale's shilly-shallying over my freedom, Rafe's lazy, careless ways. They put a venom in my veins and left hurting places. Not scars like Pa got, but bruises you can't see. Now I b'lieve I'll close my eyes and rest awhile. This gouty chest has left me purely crumpled up.

What's that chiming sound? The rain has let up, so it must be some fool at the turnstile, thinking the museum is open. You go on along downstairs, Maggie. We're not selling any tickets tonight. Tell them Peale's Museum is closed. Tell them Moses Williams said so.

Inventory of Moses Williams's Lock Box

   poplar whistle ✓

   sketch of Philis ✓

   key labeled Bear's Cage ✓

   profile of Mariah Williams ✓

   five hundred dollars in United States
currency ✓

   deed to house situated in 10 Sterling
Alley ✓

   3 pages copied from Peale's private
papers ✓

Thursday Nov. 5th 1788

Antidotes against the Poisonous effects of Arsenic, from a french work of M.P. Toussant Navier, Phisician to the King of France. For Persons who have been poisoned with arsenic he recommends <u>large quantities of milk</u>. The cure is finished by the use of <u>milk and warm sulphureous waters</u>, which experience has shown to be very powerful in removing the numbness, convulsions, and paralytic complaints, which are the constant effects of Poison.

Saturday Augt. 7th 1790

I have a suspission that by assisting to clean the Museum & brushing behind the Banks where some Arsenic might have collected by the brushing of those Birds which had been immerged in a Solution of that Poison in Water, that I might have drawn in by breathing some of the fine particles of arsenic.

I at first thought it was only a common collick & treated it as such, but my Pains in the bowels continuing after I had been worked by Castor Oil, which never before failed to cure the colick in me. _I now took some Sulpher and found myself better_, I repeated it, and I hope _by drinking milk_ and using some sope water to be cured.

C. W. P.'s Autobiography, 1826

Taxidermy is a dangerous undertaking, as standing over the fumes of the arsenical water, it must be at times drawn in with the breath.

If I had known that <u>sulphur</u> would neutralize arsenic the use of it would much sooner have restored me, as afterwards my practice to take of that valuable medicine a tea-spoon full of it whenever I felt myself indisposed, <u>it generally restored me to health</u>.

Memorandum

This memorandum verifies the contents of the lock box belonging to my father, Moses Williams, who died of slow poisoning on the fourth day of July instant. May the Lord bless him and keep him free.

Maggie Williams, eighteen years of age
Proprietor, Sterling Profiles
Philadelphia, Pennsylvania
July 7 1833

THE END

AUTHOR'S NOTE

Ten years ago I began collecting early nineteenth-century silhouettes, or profiles. Now three framed families of Philadelphia Quakers—Bonsalls, Cressens, Emlens—gaze from my bookshelf. Each profile is embossed with the words PEALE'S MUSEUM, but all are unsigned.

When I look at the hollow-cut pictures in sunlight, I can see faint tracings left by the stylus of a physiognotrace. Almost two centuries ago, a skillful profile maker ignored the lines to cut a more accurate image of each face. My curiosity about this nameless silhouettist led me to Charles Willson Peale's diaries and letters.[1] Within these thousands of pages, I discovered the fascinating story of Peale and Moses Williams.

Peale was one of America's first scientists and portrait painters. As a profile cutter in Peale's Museum, Williams was one of the earliest known African-American artists in the United States. He worked for the Peale family for fifty-one years as a slave and freedman. Yet he is mentioned only twenty-one times in Peale's vast papers.

From these brief notations, I uncovered a skeletal outline of Williams's life: The origin and names of his parents; the month and year of his birth; some of the many jobs he performed for Peale; the estimated year of his release from enslavement; and the birth of a daughter in 1808. (I named this daughter "Phoebe"; Maggie is a fictional character.) I also learned that Peale treated Williams for yellow fever with Benjamin Rush's "cure" and taught him the dangerous practice of taxidermy.

Peale's papers prove that Moses Williams was important to the operation of the museum. They also show that Peale deceived himself about slavery. Like his friend, Thomas Jefferson, the third President of the United States, Peale claimed he was opposed to bondage.

In practice, though, neither man could resist the lure of free labor. Jefferson freed only five of his more than 130 slaves. Peale freed Moses Williams after twenty-seven years of servitude. Only then could he write in his diary, "the very idea of slavery is horrible."

Peale denied the inhumanity of slavery, and so did his second son, Rembrandt. In 1858, at the age of sixty-seven, Rembrandt wrote a reminiscence. He remembered that his father manumitted the "well-known Moses" at twenty-seven. Moses then saved enough money to buy a house and eventually marry Peale's Irish cook. But until then, Charles

Willson Peale was "compelled" to keep the "entirely worthless" man enslaved because he was "too lazy to work."

"My father," recalled Rembrandt, "*insisted* on giving him his freedom one year in advance."[2]

The Peale family's ability to lie to themselves may have extended to the death of the oldest son, Raphaelle. Art historians agree that Raphaelle probably died of arsenic poisoning. They disagree about the reason.[3] One suggests that Charles Willson Peale willfully allowed Raphaelle to use arsenic so he could avoid it himself.[4] Another says Peale was not aware that Raphaelle was sick from arsenic because heavy drinking disguised his symptoms.[5] Some think Raphaelle knew arsenic was harmful, but performed taxidermy to please his father.[6]

We have no clear answer to the mystery of Raphaelle's death. Diary entries prove that Peale knew the poison was harmful. He also knew it could be fatal. A fellow scientist in Philadelphia experimented on frogs, cats, rabbits, and dogs, proving that a single grain injected into a frog could kill it within hours. Written reports of the experiments were stored at Philosophical Hall, where Charles Willson Peale was librarian.

Peale also would have read *A General System of Toxicology: Or a Treatise on Poisons*. It was published in Philadelphia in 1817, the same year that Peale wrote to Raphaelle, "My dear Raph . . . why will you neglect yourself?" The book listed the dreadful effects of arsenic when inhaled as dust and fumes over a long period of time. They included "loss of feeling in the feet and hands, delirium, falling off of the hair."[7] The author suggested a treatment similar to Peale's antidote of milk mixed with sulfur.[8]

Like most medical practices of the eighteenth century, the milk remedy was mere guesswork. It seemed to be a cure because the body quickly voided the poison through vomiting and defecation. Now doctors say symptoms of slow arsenic poisoning are unpredictable. They come and go and can appear up to thirty years after last exposure.[9]

Moses Williams was first exposed to arsenic in 1799. Twenty-eight years later, he left his job at Peale's Museum. Was he a victim of arsenic poisoning? We do not know how or when he died, only that city directories listed him as a profile cutter until 1833.[10]

Nor do we know the date of his marriage or names of his children. Charles Willson Peale noted the births, marriages, and deaths of family members and slaves on the endpapers of a dictionary. Unfortunately, the page listing information on slaves disappeared when Peale rebound the book.[11] And only five signed letters from Raphaelle Peale have been located.

Moses and Raphaelle are silent now, the true story of their deaths hidden by the passage of two hundred years. I felt it was time to give them a chance to speak for themselves. Moses, especially, deserved a fictional opportunity to repeal the offensive record left by Rembrandt.

Luckily, hundreds of Moses Williams's delicate silhouettes survive. Fifty of Raphaelle Peale's exquisite still life paintings endure, and a silhouette of Moses Williams thought to be cut by Raphaelle was discovered in 1996. This artistic legacy helps us imagine the lives of two boys, one black and one white, who grew up in the same house, controlled by the same master.

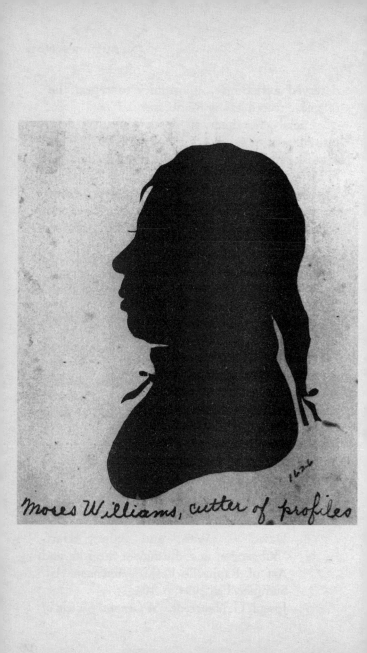

Moses Williams, cutter of profiles

NOTES

1. Lillian Miller, ed. *The Selected Papers of Charles Willson Peale and His Family* (New Haven: Yale University Press), 1983.
2. Rembrandt Peale. "Notes and Queries," *The Crayon*, 1858, pp. 307–308.
3. William H. Honan. "Suspicions of Hatred in a Family of Artists," *The New York Times* Arts Section, July 5, 1993, pp. 13, 18.
4. Phoebe Lloyd. "Philadelphia Story," *Art in America*, November 1988, p. 167.
5. Lillian Miller. "Father and Son: The Relationship of Charles Willson Peale and Raphaelle Peale," *The American Art Journal*, Volume XXV, Numbers 1 and 2, 1993, p. 51.
6. David C. Ward and Sidney Hart. "Subversion and Illusion in the Life and Art of Raphaelle Peale," *American Art*, Summer/Fall 1994, p. 104.
7. Joseph G. Nancrede. "*A General System of*

    Toxicology: Or a Treatise on Poisons (Philadelphia: M. Carey & Sons, 1817), p. 53.

8. Ibid., p. 73.

9. Phoebe Lloyd. "Arsenic, An Old Case: The Chronic Heavy Metal Poisoning of Raphaelle Peale," *Perspectives in Biology and Medicine*, Summer 1994, p. 660.

10. Stephen Jones. "A Keen Sense of the Artistic: African American Material Culture in the 19th Century," *International Review of African American Art*, Volume 12, Number 1, 1995, p. 6.

    Moses Williams's address is listed as 10 Sterling Alley in *A Directory of the Book-Arts and Book Trade in Philadelphia to 1820*, by H. Glenn Brown and Maude O. Brown (New York: New York Public Library, 1950), p. 125.

11. Telephone conversation between the author and David Ward, January 1995.

ACKNOWLEDGMENTS

I am grateful to the Virginia Foundation for the Humanities and Public Policy for a Visiting Fellowship, which allowed me to complete this book in the fall of 1995.

The following people generously answered questions or directed me to other sources:

Michael Auer, Preservation Assistance Division of the National Park Service, Washington, D.C.

Charles Blockson, Blockson Collection, Temple University, Philadelphia, PA.

Ruby Boyd and Lula Belle Hardman, Mother Bethel Church, Philadelphia, PA.

William Brookover, Chief Historical Architect, Independence National Historical Park, Philadelphia, PA.

Beth Carroll-Horrocks, American Philosophical Society, Philadelphia, PA.

Amy Fleming, Historical Society of Pennsylvania, Philadelphia, PA.

David Hart, Peale Papers, Smithsonian Institution, Washington, D.C.

Phoebe Lloyd, Texas Tech University, Lubbock, TX.

Sarah Weatherwax and Jennifer Sanchez, The Library Company of Philadelphia, Philadelphia, PA.

The floor plan of Peale's Museum at the State House (now Independence Hall) is based on maps from:

Batchelor, Penelope. "Independence Hall Historical Structures Report, Architectural Data Section: The Physical History of the Second Floor," 1992.

These people guided my excursion through *The Poison Place*: Art Collier suggested the tour; Marc Aronson turned the corners with me; Jon Lanman directed me to the exit; Jonathan and Lexie furnished the props; my husband, Paul, as always, provided the light.